You Take the High Road:
A Love Story

I hope you enjoy reading my story. I had so much fun writing it and remembering.

Loretta Wilson
(Angie)

You Take the High Road:
A Love Story

Loretta Wilson

First Printing: 2014

Second paperback edition

ISBN 978-0-692-27440-8

Loretta Wilson
Morgan Hill, CA 95037

lorettacarolynwils.wix.com/youtakethehighroad
https://www.facebook.com/youtakethehighroadnovel

Printed by www.48hrbooks.com

I dedicate this novel to my children,
Julie, Jill, and Jimmy, that they may relive the
memories of their father, but mostly, this is
a tribute to my husband, Jim,
the love of my life.

Acknowledgements

My sincere thanks goes to: my granddaughter, Alissa Wilson, for the hours and hours she spent typing, correcting my spelling, and editing my story; Anna Giubileo, Rebecca Barone and Kristie Ellington, for editing the editor; Mark Gamez for designing the cover.

Thanks to the Cliff Hangers Writers who meet at BookSmart book store. They kept me on track and critiqued my chapters. Thanks also to Renette Torres, author and new found friend.

A badge of courage goes to my sisters Linda and Anita, to my Ya-Ya friends, and to Vivian, Lucille, Kathy and John, Randy, Lisa, and all the other friends who put up with listening to me reading chapters and asking their opinions.

I mostly want to thank my children, Julie, Jill, Jimmy, and daughter-in-law, Christie, and son-in-law, Ken, for encouraging me to keep writing, being supportive, and often reminding me of incidents to add to my story that I had forgotten.

Chapter 1

1955

Having just stepped off the Loop-D-Loop, Angela Divencenzi and Judi Meiers walked through the fairway at the Santa Clara County Fair, heading toward the pavilion to listen to the blaring music. Looking around the crowd, they were hoping to see Jack and Tommy.

The two girls were seniors at the private, all-girls, Notre Dame High School and often spent their time at the youth club dances at St. Patrick's Church. Occasionally, boys from James Lick High, the public school on the eastside of San Jose, would come to the dances to check out those girls from Notre Dame, having heard rumors that those girls were fast and hot for boys. Jack and Tommy, known as the bad boys, had only attended twice. The chaperone at the dances was Fr. Flanagan, who walked around with a flash light checking to see that the students didn't dance too closely. After the "white collar" spotted them twice with his flash light, they decided that the church dance was not the place to match up with hot girls. Now, spending the day at the fair, the girls eagerly hoped they would run into the boys at some point during the day.

Judi was shorter than Angela. She was the head cheerleader at Notre Dame. She had long brown hair and braces on her teeth. Angela, tall and thin, had just gotten hers off two months earlier. The two girls were dressed identically: tight Levi's, western snap button shirts, and moccasins, with yellow ribbons around their necks. Their leather tooled belts had their names engraved on the back. Their next ride would be "The Octopus," with eight baskets twirling on the ends of its

1

arms as it went up and down, around and around. At the top of their voices they sang the words to "Round Her Neck She Wore a Yellow Ribbon."

Angie, clutched her queasy stomach and wondered, *Why didn't I stay home?*

Judi could tell that Angela wasn't feeling well, but before she could whine and wheedle her into staying a little longer, she looked to the left and noticed two guys staring at them. She quickly forgot about Jack and Tommy. These two were better looking. She poked her friend and when Angela looked up, the two guys were already walking their way. They exchanged names and Orville, the tall skinny one, asked if he and his friend, Dillon, could walk along with them, maybe treat them to a ride on the Ferris wheel.

Angela was about to decline, but Judi cut her off, saying enthusiastically that they just loved the Ferris wheel. She grabbed Orville's arm and chatted away as they climbed into the wheel's basket. Angela and Dillon were left to follow behind. They too boarded the wheel, but neither said a word. Angela kept glancing at him out of the corner of her eye. He glanced at her. When their eyes met, they quickly turned away.

The wheel completed several rounds and came to a stop. The pairs dismounted. As they walked toward the exit of the carnival ride, Angela gasped and grabbed Judi's arm as she spotted her parents coming towards them. She didn't even know the boys' last names,

Judi assured her she could handle the situation. She greeted Mr. and Mrs. Divencenzi, and made the introduction using first names only. She then hurriedly explained that they had just met these old friends, who treated them to a ride on the Ferris wheel.

Dillon nodded his head, his thumbs in the pockets of his jeans. Orville stuck out his hand, but Mr. Divencenzi ignored it.

Turning to Angela he reminded her to be at the exit on time so she wouldn't miss the last bus out. He gave the boys the evil eye, grabbed his wife's arm, and strolled off. He then whispered to Eda, his wife,

2

that he thought Judi was a bad influence on Angela and he didn't like the looks of those ruffians either.

The four teens hurried away from Angela's parents. Just like the girls, Dillon and Orville were dressed alike: Levi's riding low on their hips, no belts, snap-button shirts, leather jackets and cowboy boots. The group walked towards the food booths, where the lines were long and unorganized.

In spite of it being the end of summer, the September weather was still warm and balmy. Orville and Judi were doing all the talking. Dillon said very little, but just kept staring at Angie, and she at him.

After a half hour spent eating hot dogs and drinking cokes, Angie began to worry; they needed to leave soon. Ignoring Judi's whining, she convinced the group to start walking towards the exit. They got there just in time to see the last bus pulling away. Angie's eyes began to water, knowing how much trouble she would be in.

Orville called her "chickie" and told her not to worry; they would give her a ride home. He then went on to describe the beauty of Dillon's car, a powder blue, '52 Ford

Angie could have called her parents, but, against her better judgment, she walked along with them to the parking lot.

Judi, wanting to be seen riding in their groovy car, jumped into the front seat and snuggled up next to Dillon. He then asked her not to put her feet up on the dashboard. Shrugging, she put her feet under her and snuggled closer.

Orville grabbed Angie's hand and pulled her into the back seat. Immediately, he began to hug her and nuzzle her neck. Mentally, Angela began to call on Jesus, Mary, Joseph, and every other saint she could think of to help her. Then, to her horror, she saw that he was chewing tobacco while trying to kiss her. She slapped at his roving hand and put her other hand over her mouth. He kept calling her sweetie and telling her that most girls liked a little chew with a kiss.

Angie slid off the seat and came up on her knees behind Dillon's seat and pleaded with him to let her come up front with him. Dillon quickly gave out the command for Judi to climb back with Orville. It made no difference to her and she flopped over the seat into Orville's waiting arms and they began kissing passionately all arms and legs intertwined.

So relieved to have escaped that situation, Angela could only say, "Thank you," as she climbed over the seat next to Dillon. She sat with both feet on the floor, hands folded in her lap. Neither of them spoke until Angie gave him the address of her house. In a quiet voice she said, "636 North 16th Street."

As soon as they pulled up to the house, Dillon came around to open the passenger door and walked Angie to her front porch. The porch light was on and the two just stood there.

She thought he was so handsome with a golden tan and white blond hair, kind of long and messy, with one piece falling over his forehead. She thought his eyes were sparkling blue, although she couldn't really see the color. She didn't think he was very tall, maybe 5'10", but she noticed his shoulders were wide. *Oh my.*

He thought her hair was beautiful: auburn, long and thick. Her eyes were light brown with lots of yellow, like cat eyes. Looking her up and down, he could see that she was kind of skinny. He could call her "my lean baby."

Just then the porch light flicked on and off, on and off, and then on again. Dillon asked if he could see her again, telling her they could go to the drive-in theater or go to Spivey's for a coke.

Angie nodded her head yes, but told him that first he must meet her parents so they could give her permission to go out with him. She invited him to come to Saturday night dinner at 5:00.

Angie watched him walk back to his car, his white blonde hair blowing in the wind. Almost to the car, Dillon turned around and smiled, "By the way, my last name is McCandless.

Angela's heart was pounding. Ta-dum. Ta-dum. Ta-dum. *Oh my.*

Angie   Judi

636 N. 16th Street, San Jose,
Angie's House

Dillon

Chapter 2

"Serafina, get out of the bathroom, NOW! Papa still has to shave." Eda Divencenzi's public image was genteel, soft spoken, sweet, never giving any opinions, deferring to her husband; the perfect politician's wife. Within the domain of her home, however, Eda reigned supreme: the commander-in-chief. Her voice raised an octave as she told Angela to stop looking for her shoes. She would find them under the table, so she should get off her knees and save the kneeling for church. Eda then tried to get Laetitia to stop wiggling, so she could fix her French braid, asking her if she wanted to look pretty for Grandmother. Laetitia shot back, "No! Grandmamma doesn't even like me!" The struggling little girl also told her mother she was not her sweet little baby. Six year old Laetitia was named after Grandmother Divencenzi as an apology for being another girl.

Americo "Rico" Divencenzi stood in the bathroom in his shorts, lathering his face with the door open. Laetitia pushed past to piddle beside him. Living with four females in a home with one small bathroom, he was oblivious to the goings on. Facing himself in the mirror, his hand would occasionally fly up as he practiced his latest speech. Some days after dinner, he would go back to City Hall for an emergency meeting with councilmen and the Board of Supervisors, discussing the expansion of San Jose.

Rico had served as councilman for 15 years. He loved this town and he loved helping San Jose develop into a large major city in central California. Being first generation Italian, he kept fellowship with the Italian neighborhood, building his house in "Little Italy" near 13th Street and Backesto Park, which had the best Bocce Ball courts in town. Across the street was his mother's house, where he grew up. He had a thriving insurance business, selling insurance to most of the Italians, often paying their premiums when they were short of funds. He was thought of as a living saint and highly respected.

Walking past the bathroom door, Eda asked Rico to go pick up his mother since the polenta and chicken cacciatore were almost ready. She had even made cannoli for dessert in an attempt to please her mother-in-law. Mama Divencenzi disliked her daughter-in-law, criticizing most everything she did, while she gushed over her son. She sympathized with him, thinking that his wife didn't take very good care of him.

Eda continued her commands as she fussed about the house, telling Serafina to set the table for seven since Angela was having a guest for dinner. She then warned Laetitia that she better behave herself or she would make her sit next to Grandmother.

Angela wore a starched white blouse and a plaid skirt. She was so nervous about tonight. She wanted them to like Dillon and she wanted him to like her family. Fat chance. That was asking far too much. Her family was so overpowering they would likely scare him off. Standing in the kitchen, she jumped when the doorbell rang and ran to the door. On the wall the clock read 5:00 pm exactly.

Answering the door, Angie motioned for Dillon to come in and took his jacket.

"Angie," he nodded his head as he removed his leather jacket. "Thanks." Again, they simply stood there, staring at each other. He was dressed in his usual snap-button shirt, Levi's, boots, leather jacket. Angie reacted first and began to babble.

"Can I get you something to drink? Coke, or maybe a glass of milk?" she asked, leading him into the dining room. The room was small, holding only two major pieces of furniture: a long table and chairs, and a piano with its bench. An arched doorway led into the living room with a large stone fireplace. "Dinner's almost ready. We're having chicken cacciatore. You'll like it. Or maybe you won't," she second guessed herself. "It's pretty spicy. But you'll definitely like dessert, cannoli, or maybe you won't like those either." She took a big breath. "Oh, just make believe you like everything, okay?" she finished.

"Everything will be fine, Angel," he reassured her quietly.

"Oh, please don't call me that. My father won't like it."

"Hiya, handsome." Her older sister Serafina entered, walked around Dillon, and looked him up and down. "Pretty cute, Sissy." Serafina was tall and beautiful, favoring her father's looks, dark hair and soulful eyes.

"Please Sera, don't make this harder—." Angela looked mortified.

Dillon smiled at Sera, a wide toothy smile. Right off, he liked her, recognizing her spunky personality.

Laetitia came next, hopping up and down, "How come your hair is almost white? Are you old?" Dillon smiled again, and leaned down towards Laetitia.

"Yeah, I guess I am old, but I don't need a cane yet." Laetitia giggled.

"That's good. You know what? Wait 'til you meet Grandmamma. She's really old. You won't like her. Do you like me?"

"Yeah, Laetitia, I do kind of like you."

"Laetitia, remember what I told you. Behave yourself." Eda came in from the kitchen and began wiping her hands on her apron. "Come in, Dillon. We can sit down now. Sit, sit." She pointed to a chair. "You sit here, next to Rico. Angela you sit next to Dillon. Your father and Grandmother will be here in a few minutes. Do you like polenta?" Eda was short, barely 5'1", and a little plump, probably from all the Italian cooking. Her face was kind; friendly with lots of laugh lines and deep dimples. Her hair was auburn and she had yellow brown cat eyes, just like Angie's.

"I don't know, ma'am. I've never had it, but I'm sure I will. Angie says you're a great cook."

Just then, Rico came into the dining room holding open the swinging door that led from the kitchen. He ushered in his mother and sat her down directly across from Dillon. He took his seat at the head of the table with Dillon on his right. Rico was impeccably dressed as always: starched white shirt, cuff links, dark blue suit and tie. He even wore his suit when he barbequed. He was tall, towering over Eda. His dark hair was traditionally combed with a part to one side. He had classic features: straight nose, thin lips, very handsome. His hands were large with long tapered fingers. He wore a signet ring on his right hand and no wedding band. Dillon stood up to greet him.

"Good to see you Dillon. Sit down." He did not offer a handshake.

Across the table Grandmother Divencenzi was not quite as tall as Rico, but she was just as stately. A very vain woman, everyone knew she padded her clothes with old nylons, especially around the hips to round them out. At church she would often flutter her eyes at some much younger men, flirting with them, much to Eda's embarrassment.

Unsmiling and without introduction, she asked Dillon, "What part of Italy is your family from?" Dillon blinked, taken aback.

"Ma'am, my father was born in Scotland. My last name is McCandless. I'm not Italian."

"Then I take it you're not Catholic either."

"No ma'am. My family didn't much attend church. But when my mother was alive, she always read the Bible. She always kept it on the kitchen table."

"Humph, Bible thumpers." That was the end of all the conversation with Dillon. Eda chatted away happily about anything and everything and nothing. After this had gone on awhile and they grazed on the antipasta of cheese, crackers, olives, and salami, Eda, Serafina, and Angela excused themselves and went into the kitchen. They returned through the swinging door carrying the food—lots of food. Alongside the main course there were always several seasonal cooked vegetables, and a big bowl of crisp green salad.

As soon as the food was set down, Dillon began to raise his wrists up to join hands like he used to do with his mom, but he dropped them quickly as all the Divencenzi's began the sign of the cross. *"In the name of the Father, Son, and Holy Ghost, bless us O'Lord, and these Thy gifts which we are about to receive from Thy bounty, through Christ our Lord, Amen."*

Then the food began to make a circle around the table. Dillon wondered if he was supposed to take some of everything on his plate, so he watched Rico and followed what he did. As he looked at all the food, the polenta puzzled him. It looked like yellow baby mush, but then the sauce and chicken were plopped on top. It tasted pretty good. Dillon glanced over at Laetitia. She had her hand up to her mouth and behind her hand she was sticking her tongue out at her grandmother.

After dinner was over the girls cleared the table. They brought out the cannoli and a variety of fruit. As the cannoli were passed around, Rico reached into his pocket and pulled out a stiletto. Dillon's head jerked back as he snapped open the blade. He was mesmerized as Rico began to peel an orange. Around and around, he peeled it all in one piece. He then offered each person around the table a segment of orange on the end of his stiletto.

Dinner was at least an hour long affair.

Wow, this is one weird family, thought Dillon, and then he glanced to the side at Angela. Her eyebrows were raised, pleading with him to be understanding. That's all it took. They could be as weird as they wanted, as long as he could keep looking at "Angel."

"Do you think we can go now Angie?" he whispered as quietly as he could.

"Let's just wait 'til Papa leaves," she whispered back, "then we can ask Mama about going to the show."

Rico and Grandmother ignored Dillon. When all the conversation died down, Rico rose. He walked over and kissed Eda's cheek and headed for the door. They all watched him go. "I'll be home around ten."

"Did you like the polenta, Mama?" asked Eda, looking back towards the table.

"It was okay, but you know I keep telling you 'not too much garlic.' It makes it too spicy. Maybe one day you'll be a true Italian cook."

Eda rolled her eyes. "I'll try to remember that, Mama."

Serafina and Angela gave Grandmother a perfunctory kiss goodbye. Laetitia hung back until Grandmother pinched her arm.

"Thank you so much for the dinner, Mrs. Divencenzi," Dillon said sincerely. 'It was really good." He hesitated. "Can I take Angie to the show?" *Good strategy* he thought. *First the compliment, then the request.*

"Of course." Eda was beaming from the dinner compliment. "You'll have to come see us again, Dillon. I'll fix you some ravioli next time."

"Thank you so much, ma'am. I'll be sure to stop by again soon." Angie hustled Dillon out of the dining room as fast as she could. "Have a good evening," he called out as he was hurried through the swinging door to the kitchen and out the back door.

Soon enough they were driving off to the drive-in. Dillon turned on the radio. Saturday Night Rosary Hour blared out.

Damn not again, thought Dillon. "You know, I used to date this Catholic girl and every time she heard them praying, she brought out her rosary beads and started praying out loud. Used to freak me out. I hope you're not a fan of the rosary."

"Well, I do pray the rosary, not as often as I should, but I do love my faith, especially Holy Mass." Angela reached over and changed the radio station and found Chubby Checkers playing "The Twist." Dillon patted the seat next to him. She moved over closer to him, and he put his arm lightly around her shoulders and drove with his left arm.

When they had reached the drive-in theater, they parked in one of the last rows. After Dillon adjusted the speakers on the window, he put his arms tightly around her and just kept looking at her. For the first time he noticed a tiny mole, high up on  her left cheek. He wondered if she had painted it on and ran a finger over it. Everything about her fascinated him.

"You make me really nervous when you just keep looking at me. Do you want to kiss me?"

"What do you think? I wanted to kiss you, first time I saw you. You're just so beautiful" He touched the sides of her face. Her heart was beating wildly. He looked her in the eyes.

And so he kissed her. Sometimes her neck, her forehead, her eyes, her cheek, but mostly her mouth. They kissed and kissed, until his hands began to roam closer to her breasts.

"Dillon, stop. We had better go to Spivey's now and then home, so I get there before Papa." He stopped, but just stared hard at her for several more minutes. The movie was only half over when he pulled the car out of the row and drove off.

Spivey's was only a few blocks away. They arrived quickly, not saying much on the short drive there. A girl on roller skates came up to the car, attached a tray to the window, and took their order. Dillon and Angela sat close to each other, and waited for their French fries to come.

Sipping their drinks a little while later, Dillon asked her, "Will you always tell me to stop?"

"I probably will, 'cause I won't do any impure acts before marriage. That would be a mortal sin."

"What a lot of hogwash!" Dillon reached under the seat and brought out a small bottle of brandy. He poured a little bit into his coke and offered some to Angela. She shook her head and he slid it back under his seat.

Desperately she raised her voice, "You don't know how I was raised. I can't do what I know is wrong."

He didn't answer her but was secretly plotting his strategy. *I really like her; maybe I could even love her already. I know she likes me too and soon she will let me do a little more than just a kiss and she won't tell me to stop 'cause I'll make sure she likes it.* Surprised by what he had just thought, he wondered, *did I really think I could love her already? I hardly know her!*

After crumbling up the wrappers and paper cups and giving the tray back to the waitress, they pulled away from Spivey's and drove home in silence. At the door, the porch light was already starting to flick on and off. Angie was so confused. She really liked Dillon, but he scared her too. He seemed so sure of himself and what he wanted. *Tonight was a disaster.* It made her sad to think that he might not ask her out again.

When they reached the door, he grabbed her and gave her a torrid kiss. Before he let her go, his hand lightly brushed her breast on purpose. She didn't mind too much. He touched her face. He wanted to touch all of her.

"I'll call you." As Dillon walked back to his car, she again noticed his white blond hair blowing in the wind.

Angela's heart pounded crazily as she watched him drive away. Ta-dum. Ta-dum. Ta-dum. *Oh my.*

13

Loretta Wilson

Rico Divencenzi   Eda Divencenzi

Chapter 3

On Sunday morning, Angela got dressed early. She walked quickly the three blocks through Backesto Park, over to the Church of the Holy Cross on 13th street. Confessions were heard half an hour before mass.

Her mind was reeling as she pondered, *What to say, what to say.* She entered the confessional box and waited. Soon a little 12" x 12" door slid open between her and the priest sitting on the other side of the wall. She knelt on the kneelers and got close to the little open screen door. She always went to Father Gereski, the Polish priest, who spoke very little English, but understood enough.

Holy Cross was mainly an Italian parish, but because of the shortage of priests, he was sent to help the pastor serve the Italian congregation.

In his thick accent, he asked her to begin her confession. Angela began, asking a blessing for she had sinned and declaring how long it had been since her last confession. She then started the usual list of routine sins, starting with having a fight with her sister. Then came the use of a swear word or expression of anger at her father. Then softly she owned up to an impure act, quickly adding that she was truly sorry and asked for forgiveness and absolution.

If she had gone to Father Salvatore, he would have grilled her about the impure act, loud enough for the whole church to hear. Instead, kindly Fr. Gereski just said, "I absolve thee in the name of the Father, the Son, and the Holy Ghost," making the sign of the cross and blessing her. "For your penance say three Hail Marys, three Our Fathers and one Glory Be. Now say the Act of Contrition."

It was over. Breathing a sigh of relief, she told God she was heartily sorry for having offended Him.

When she had finished, Fr. Gereski dismissed her saying "Go in peace. Sin no more." Angela released a big breath and moved out of the box, up the aisle to her favorite pew in front of the rows of votive candles. She knelt and lit one and prayed that Dillon still liked her, but *Please God, make him behave chastely.* She then recited her penance prayers and experienced the peaceful feeling she always had after Confession.

The church was still dark with only the candles for light. She glanced at the thick altar rail with the white cloth over it. She loved to put the cloth up under her chin when she took Communion. She looked up at the huge crucifix above the altar. "Thank you, Jesus."

The lights came on in the church. Holy Mass would soon begin.

Along with Saturday night dinner with Grandmother Divencenzi, Sunday lunch with Grandma and Grandpa Savio was another tradition. Every Sunday around noon, the entire family would drive out to their ranch.

I'm never bringing Dillon here. He'll really think my family is crazy, Angela decided as they pulled up to the house after church that Sunday. Besides her family, there was Aunt Elsie and Uncle Fred Bertaccini and their twin sons, Ed and Fred. After them came Aunt Evelina and Uncle Bill Murphy, whom the family just called "The Irishman." They had no children. Then there was Aunt Josephina with her third husband, Marco Zappia. They called him "The Gambler," because no one knew what he did for a living other than frequent the card rooms. She too, had no children.

Tiny Grandma Savio spoke no English. She never left the ranch, always cooking for the hired hands and taking care of her child with

Down syndrome. Grandpa even cut her light brown hair, there on the ranch, which she wore parted down the middle and straight around her face, ending just below her ears. She was very fair, with blue eyes, having come from Piedmont, Northern Italy.

Grandpa did all the shopping and farmed a 40-acre walnut tree orchard. He was not very tall, with short legs and a muscular upper body, but his girth was at least 50 inches around. From 12:00 to 3:00 he played pinochle with his four sons-in-law, three of whom were afraid of him and cringed at his booming voice. They always let him win. He kept a whiskey bottle on the table with little shot glasses, and the more he drank, the louder he got.

Rico saw through all his bluster. He mostly let him win too, but once in a while he'd win a hand, just to rile him. When the card game ended, Grandpa would scoop up the money and head for his bedroom, leaving the door open enough so all could see what he was doing. There was the big black safe. Down on his knees, he put the money inside. Years late, after he died, everyone thought the safe would be full of money. Instead there was only the deed to the ranch, which made little Grandma a very wealthy woman. The city annexed the ranch, making it part of the downtown desirable area.

Eda and her three sisters, Josephina, Evelina, and Elsie, helped prepare the lunch. Food, food, and more food. Grandma's specialty was gnocchi served with a white sauce. Northern Italy had a French influence; pasta sauces were white, although she sometimes gave in and served the hearty Sicilian red sauce over pasta. The vegetable soup was served first, then gnocchi, baked chicken with little roasted potatoes, and more vegetables. Last was the green salad with olive oil and red wine vinegar dressing. Dessert was panettone with fresh slices of fruit, and red wine to drink with a little Galliano after lunch.

Everyone remained at the table while Grandpa told stories about Italy and coming to New York. His father had sent for him to come to America, but during the two-month-long boat trip over, his father had died. He had arrived, 12 years old and speaking no English, with no one to meet him when he got off the ship. After wandering the streets alone and hungry, Mother Cabrini found him and took him in until he was 16 years old. Then he went off on his own, working on the docks or in the restaurants. He learned the restaurant business and soon opened his own restaurant. He would sing opera to the patrons while they ate. The business was thriving until they built the elevated train above the restaurant. The noise killed all possibility of success.

He then wrote to Mary, his childhood friend back in Italy: "Mary, come to me. We will get married and go to California and farm. The weather there is like Italy. New York is too cold."

Grandpa sometimes got teary reminiscing. He embellished the story, depending on how much liquor he had drunk. That afternoon Grandpa Savio was particularly intoxicated, wildly recounting story after story. He spoke of going to the junk yard on Saturday mornings. If there was a surplus of windows, he would buy all they had. When he had enough, he then built a little house to fit the windows. Eventually he had a row of rental houses on the ranch. In addition to the orchard, he grew produce, and then organized other farmers to form a wholesale farmers' produce market, controlling the price.

He looked around the table at his family and began to share his favorite story about Prohibition.

"Me, Giuseppe Savio," he said, pointing to himself, "was the largest distributor of wine during the prohibition in Santa Clara County. The story continued, "At night, son-in-law Fred would park the cars in the orchard. I had celebrities come from Hollywood to buy my wine. Even Laurel and Hardy came. Tuesday night was reserved for the lady telephone operators who came to play cards and drink my wine. Ma Na! Could those women drink!"

Angie began to zone out, as Grandpa talked on and on. Her mind wandered back to when she and Serafina often spent weekends out at the ranch. Grandpa Savio would let them suck on the hoses to get the wine flowing. She also remembered how he threw her in the chicken coop when she had picked his prized onion seed plant. The chickens were flapping and she was screaming until little Grandma rescued her. They loved to play in the orchard with their twin cousins, Ed and Fred. They would tip the wine barrels over, get inside the huge empty vats, and get them rolling, or they would wade through the water and mud irrigation ditches bare-footed. On Saturdays Grandpa would take his two granddaughters to Alum Rock Park to get jugs of spring and sulfur water, and then he would take them to the movies. Never minding what was playing, he wanted the free dishes that the Victory Theater gave away. Angela shuddered, recalling some of the horror films they saw.

When her focus returned to the table, Grandpa was finishing up his last story of the afternoon. As always, when he got tired of talking, he called for Mary to untie his shoes: it was time for his nap. They'd both walked to the bedroom and he would lie down, while she knelt on the little prayer bench at the foot of the bed.

Angela loved to hear her when she knelt there and prayed out loud in Italian. She knew Grandma wasn't saying the usual prayers; she was talking to God. How she wished she could understand the words.

Then it was time to go home. The dishes were washed, the kitchen had been cleaned, and Grandpa was snoring loudly. Grandma gave everyone a kiss and placed a quarter in each of the grandchildren's hands. They always wondered where she got the quarters.

Just as the Divencenzi family arrived back home the phone began to ring. Angela rushed to answer it.

"When can I see you, Angel?"

"I can't go out during the school week. I have to study."

"Does it take all week to study?" Dillon sounded disappointed.

"Usually. Daddy expects us to get all As."

"Jesus, I'm in love with a genius?"

"Not likely, but I can see you Saturday afternoon."

"Wear your Levi's, Angel. I have something special in mind."

(above) Twin cousins, Ed and Fred Bertaccini. Grandma and Grandpa Savio, Angie and Serafina

(right) Serafina, Aunt Evalina, Angie, and Laetitia

(below) Grandpa and Grandma Savio, Grandma Divencenzi, at Angie's christening

Chapter 4

Angie thought that if she kept very busy the week would go by faster. She aggressively attacked her closet, filling bags with unused clothes to donate to the St. Vincent De Paul Society and rearranging remaining items by color. Her dresser drawer got dumped onto her bed and underwear got refolded. She even vacuumed under the bed and washed her hair twice in one day.

All week, she had difficulty studying and—God forbid—she got a B on a test that she thought she had studied for. Several times in class she caught herself staring out the window, not listening.

Dillon called every day with not too much to say. He just wanted to hear her voice and then wondered why he was so obsessed with her.

Each morning before school, Angie continued to make her daily early morning trek to Church of the Holy Cross. She enjoyed the walk through their neighborhood, especially in the spring, often humming her favorite song or sometimes running part of the way there, passing the homes of their tightly knit community.

Rico had built their house in Little Italy the year Angela was born. Their 16th Street block between Jackson and Taylor Streets was teeming with families. All the Italian mothers watched out for each and every kid. There was Mrs. Chirco, Mrs. Forni, Mrs. Cardone, Mrs. Blasé and Mrs. Cancilla, always keeping an eye on the kids.

In summer, the children would play dodge ball in the street until late at night and, in the winter, small tables were set up in one of the garages where a continuous game of Monopoly would be played sitting on prune crates.

Claudette, Diane, Joanie, Joycie, Beverly, Eddie, Kenny, Michael and Jo'Ann, and the other neighborhood kids were always in each other's company. There was no shortage of these life-long friends. In mid-summer, the nearby ranchers made a sweep through the neighborhood, driving a flatbed truck, picking up whoever wanted to go cut apricots, even those too young to have work permits. The children were told that if the labor commissioner showed up, they were to disappear out into the orchard until he left.

Among the kids, the competition was to see how many trays they could stack up before the "tray-boys" took them away to be placed in the sulfur house and then out to be sun dried.

Most of the time, they cut with a knife, but sometimes the apricots were so ripe that the pit was squeezed out and the fruit was slapped on the tray. These were called slabs; they made the best dried fruit, full of sugar. The cutters were happy to get their hands sloppy with apricot juice as the trays were filled quickly.

There was one nosy neighbor, Carmine Bevalacqua; he gave Angie the creeps, always watching her walk to church every day. He would shout out to her mom, "Hey, Eda, what does that daughter of yours do that's so bad she has to go to church every day?"

"Better church, Carmine, than the likes of your daughter, going carousing downtown every night."

At the last house on the block lived Mrs. Goldberg, the only Jewish lady among the Italians. The other women did not associate with her and Angie always wondered why. She was so friendly, always waving to Angie as she passed her house on the way to church. Occasionally, she could hear Mrs. Goldberg's daughter, Esther, practicing her violin early in the morning. Esther never came out of the house to play. Angie always forgot to ask mama about them.

Other than Mr. Bevalacqua, it was an ideal and happy neighborhood to grow up in. And each day, rain or shine, Angie would continue to walk through it on her way to church.

After walking past the homes of her neighbors and friends, she walked through Backesto Park, then into the cold, dark church and up the aisle to kneel in her favorite pew. Candles burned and the faint smell of incense drifted through the church. Angie could say all the mass prayers without looking at her daily missal. The ritual ended with Communion over the white altar cloth and, after waving to Fr. Gereski, she would head for home. That morning, she wondered if he knew she was the one who committed the impure act.

Back at her house, a hearty breakfast was always waiting for her, and she would join her sisters at the table to enjoy a meal together. Laetitia dressed in a starched white middy with a navy tie and navy pleated skirt; Serafina and Angela dressed in long, black, serge jumpers, white blouses, black string ties, black and white saddle shoes and nylons. The three sisters and some of the other neighborhood kids would then climb into the backseat of the family's car, dressed in their freshly washed and ironed uniforms, ready for Papa to drive them to school.

Rico sometimes forgot they were back there. He was frequently so engrossed in his next speech, waving his arms and talking out loud, that the kids would laugh and duck down behind the seat, just to see how far he would take them toward his office before he remembered to take them to St. Patrick's grade school and Notre Dame High. He also routinely forgot a particular stop sign on the route, and the policeman routinely reminded him, "Mr. Divencenzi, the stop sign is still there."

"Oh, I know, officer, I'll remember. Have a nice day. Thank you, officer." There was little traffic there, and when he showed him his city council badge, no ticket was given.

Rico was very involved at the girl's high school, accepting the duty of being president of the Dad's Club. He arranged for educational tours, chaperoned the snow trips, and organized the father/daughter dance. Serafina and Angela were embarrassed to see their principal, Sister Mary Delarosa, blush and stammer when she talked to Rico. She actually batted her eyes at him. He was so handsome, a polite and charming gentleman. All the nuns loved him.

Rico worked at his office half a day on Saturdays. Angela often went with him to dust his office and file papers, for which she was paid $2.00 in addition to her weekly allowance. This Saturday, she would not be joining him.

Angie told Eda she was going to take Dillon to the park since the "Yo-yo Man" was going to be giving demonstrations. Then she was going to teach Dillon how to play tennis. She left out the part about Dillon having a surprise for her.

Dillon arrived a little after noon. Angie took special care in dressing in her best western shirt and Levi's, a scarf around her neck and her hair tied in a ponytail.

When she answered the door, the staring began, with Dillon devouring every inch of her, up and down. She was pleased to see his smile of approval. She stared back, concentrating on his handsome face, especially his magical eyes. "Where are we going, Dillon?"

"You'll see. Grab a jacket, Angel, and let's go."

At the car, he threw the tennis rackets in the back. "No girly games for me."

Two blocks away, chained to a telephone pole, was an old Indian motorcycle. Dillon parked his Ford, unchained the Indian and climbed on. "Come on, Angel, we're going for a ride. Throw your leg over and hang on."

Never in her life had Angie done anything so reckless. Her heart was pounding, this time, from fear. Without a backward glance, she grabbed Dillon tightly around the waist, put her cheek on his back, and shut her eyes.

The roar was deafening. He gunned the engine and they took off. She was sure they were traveling faster than the legal limit. It felt so good to hold on to Dillon. She squeezed him tighter, knowing she was safe.

When she finally got up the nerve to raise her head to look around, giggles bubbled out of her and a smile spread across her face. She wanted to shout, "Look at me! Oh, mamma mia, look at me!"

Traveling over Hecker Pass on their way to the ocean, Dillon reminded her to lean with him on the curves. Oh, she felt like such a professional motorcycle rider.

They were heading for Boulder Creek, a coastal town with a deep forest. All around were the tall redwood trees, not letting in much sun, keeping it cool most of the time.

Stopping off at a stream, he showed her how to cup her hands to get a drink of the ice cold water. Neither seemed inclined to talk, content to sit on a rock, soak up the shadowy scenery, and continue to stare at each other.

Oh, his eyes really were blue, dark blue, with a darker circle around the pupil, kind of like the eyes Angie had seen on a Siberian husky. Almost scary, hypnotizing eyes, especially when he stared at her. But he was so handsome, and her heart began its rapid beat.

Dillon talked very little, mostly asking questions. They hardly knew anything about each other. All Angie really knew was that he lived with his father in the small town of Morgan Hill, twenty miles south of San Jose. Their 20-acre parcel of land was just below the huge mountain called Murphy's Peak, also sometimes referred to as El Toro, or as his father nicknamed it, Gobbler's Nob. The land was leased out to Japanese farmers to grow strawberries.

"Someday, I'll take you for a walk up the mountain. There's a trail past the water tank clean to the top. There's even a cave up there that some claim Joaquin Murietta hid out in. You can see for miles around from the top." Angie loved listening to his deep voice talking about his town. She could hear the prideful connection he had with Morgan Hill.

Back on the bike, they slowly rode home. Angie would always remember that trip and the day she fell in love.

He re-chained the Indian bike; his friend Earl would pick it up later. The two rode off in his blue '52 Ford.

Dillon's love of his car was evident; everything was highly polished, not a scratch or speck of dust anywhere. Heading in the direction of home, he suddenly pulled off the road and drove deep into a nearby orchard of trees.

"Dillon, what are you doing?" Angie squeaked as they bounced over the furrows of dirt.

"I really need to kiss you," was his only explanation. Stopping the car, he grabbed her tightly and kissed her passionately.

She loved his clean scent, leather with a touch of Old Spice. She kissed him back. He exhaled deeply, sat back, wondering why he could not get enough of her. Why was he always thinking of her? She was making him crazy with her "Stop, Dillon," attitude. Why couldn't she be like Tomasina, his old girlfriend, who wouldn't stop at anything, or like Irma? He had lost his virginity to her in the dirt under the big oak tree at the back of the ranch. He smiled remembering. *Oh, sweet Irma. She taught me so much.*

He grabbed Angie again for another kiss. She loved kissing him, but when his breathing quickened, she squeaked out, "Stop, Dillon."

Reaching under the seat, he got out his bottle of brandy, and took a big swig, hoping it would cool down his brain and other parts. When his breathing returned to normal, he turned on the ignition and drove her home in silence. Angela's heart was still racing as they turned down her street. Ta-dum. Ta-dum. Ta-dum. *Oh my.*

If weather permitted, they drove over to Santa Cruz to walk on the boardwalk. Only the merry-go-round was running in the winter and Angie always took a ride. Dillon didn't even consider climbing on a wooden horse.

Week after week, for the next three months, their romance continued along the same pattern: drive-in movie or park in an orchard in the middle of winter. Getting stuck in the mud, they once had to call Dillon's friend Earl to tow the car out.

Worse than getting his car all muddy, was the fact that Angela, with mud up to her ankles, had taken Serafina's new white Spalding shoes without asking. Ruined forever, even the buck bag could not restore them. She had to turn over her allowance and the extra two dollars she got from Papa for three months.

The kisses continued, and now she allowed a little breast caressing, but that was all!

"Stop, Dillon." Out came the brandy bottle. Then came confession, forgive me Father, penance prayers, go in peace, sin no more.

It bothered her that she knew she would sin again, but she could hardly wait to see Dillon each week.

Angie sitting on Dillon's
'52 Ford

Chapter 5

1956

In January, on a Friday night, a man called asking to speak to Angela Divencenzi. Serafina handed her the phone and instantly grabbed Angie's hand, sensing this call was serious. She stayed close hoping she could hear the conversation.

"This is Jacob McCandless, Dillon's father. I don't want to alarm you, but Dillon's been in an accident. He was hit by a truck riding his motorcycle. His injuries are not life threatening, but there was considerable damage done to his leg. Both the truck and motorcycle pulled into the middle lane, turning in opposite directions and they collided. Those damn three lane roads! Now you know why they call Monterey Highway 'Blood Alley.'" He sounded bitter but also scared. "Dillon's at Wheeler Hospital in Gilroy, ten miles south of Morgan Hill. Before he went into surgery he asked me to call you. I'll keep you posted."

Sera hugged Angie. "I'll pray for him."

Angie relayed to Eda what Jacob had told her. "Mama I have to go to him. Please make Papa understand."

Eda saw the determined look on her daughter's face and realized at once that she was surely in love with this young man.

"I'll talk to Papa and get his permission for you to go. Go pack a bag and then he can drive you to the bus station. He'll understand."

Well, he didn't understand. "She's too young to be in love."

"And how old were we?"

"Things were different then with the war starting."

"Rico, Rico. Age has nothing to do with matters of the heart."

Reluctantly, he kissed her cheek, gave Angie five dollars, drove her to the station, and stayed with her 'til she boarded the bus.

"Give my best to Dillon."

Angie arrived late at night and gained entrance through the emergency door. It was a small hospital, probably only twenty beds, and she easily found his room. She tip-toed in. There was a small light on above his bed. Tears filled her eyes when she saw him unconscious and connected to IV tubes and oxygen. She held his hand, kissed his forehead and settled into the chair next to the bed. All through the night, she continued to hold his hand and prayed. *Please God, let him be alright.*

She slept off and on and came fully awake early the next morning as she heard someone shuffling and coughing coming down the hall towards Dillon's room. Dr. Jenkins wore his green surgical hat and gown. A cigarette dangled from his mouth. He coughed again, surprised to see Angie sitting there.

"Well, what have we here? Where did you come from little lady? Who are you?"

"I'm Angela Divencenzi. Dillon is my boyfriend. I just had to come see him. Please tell me he'll be alright. Why doesn't he wake up?"

Dr. Jenkins put his cigarette out in the urinal next to the bed, coughed a phlegmy cough and lit up another. He began checking Dillon's leg and adjusting the tubes. "Oh, he'll wake up soon enough, but he'll wish he was back unconscious. He was banged up pretty bad, lots of bruises and lacerations. Those will get better. I'm doing my best to save his leg. He has multiple fractures up the leg and ankle. I'm keeping him sedated to give him time to heal. I'll check on him tomorrow. Stay here with him if you like. At least this will keep him out of the draft." He made notations on Dillon's chart and patted Angie on the shoulder. "He'll be glad to see you." He shuffled out coughing and wheezing.

Angela kept her vigil all day and the next night in the dark room.

Coming back from the bathroom she saw those piercing blue eyes staring at her. "Have I died and gone to heaven, 'cause I see an angel coming in."

Her emotions exploded. She ran to the bed, flinging herself on his bare chest, wetting his face with her tears, kissing him all over. "You have to get well." She was blubbering and hiccupping. He winced in pain as she began shaking his shoulders. "Please Dillon, you have to get well." Sobbing softly she lay her head back on his chest.

Slurring his words, Dillon spoke again, "This was worth getting hit by a truck." Then he was back asleep.

When Sunday night came, he was still asleep. She kissed him goodbye, hugged him gently this time and headed out to the bus station. For Angie, it would be a long, long week before she could come back.

രജ്ഞ

The doctors decided that Dillon needed to be kept hospitalized for at least four weeks. As soon as all the cuts and lacerations were healed, a full cast was put on from his ankle to his hip. The leg was then placed in a sling and attached to the ceiling.

Immediately after her last class Friday afternoons, Angela rushed to the bus station to get to the hospital. The nurses were glad to see her as she took over his care completely for the weekends.

Best of all, Dillon and Angie had plenty of time to truly get to know each other, learning about each other's likes and dislikes. They laughed a lot and Angie would read to him. She fussed and fussed over him, straightening his blankets and fluffing his pillows.

He mostly liked all the attention until the day she tried to feed him and wipe his mouth. He pushed her hand aside, harder than he should have. "I'm not a baby. Cut it out."

Angie said nothing, but calmly collected her purse and the box of candy she had brought him, walked out and went home.

Now I've done it, thought Dillon. *What's the matter with me? Treating her like that.*

Alone for the rest of the weekend, he began reminiscing about his childhood. No one had ever fussed over him. He hardly knew his mother. He was only five years old when his much older brother went off to war. He had seen pictures of him: tall, well built, blonde with an infectious smile. His father had told him that girls called him "Flash Gordon" because he had those good looks and a devil-may-care personality.

Dillon's mother spent all her time worrying about his brother. After he had been deployed for some time, the family received news that his plane had crashed over the ocean and his body was never found. Refusing to accept reality, his mother continued to wait for his return. She fell into a deep depression and eventually needed to be hospitalized. Jacob sought help from many doctors, but none could make his wife accept the loss of her first born son. Wishing to shield son from his mother's condition, Jacob refused to bring Dillon with him to visit his mother in the hospital. She died only a year after her son went missing.

Jacob did the best he could raising Dillon. He had to work two jobs, struggling to pay for the remaining medical bills and the home he cared for. As a consequence, Dillon mostly grew up alone with just his dog, Freckles, at home. His father depended on the Japanese sharecroppers to keep an eye on him. As young as he was, he knew how to make miracle whip sandwiches for lunch and Jacob made macaroni and cheese dinners. They rarely ate any vegetables.

31

Dillon thought again about why he was pushing Angie out of his life. *She'd be better off without me. She'll surely leave me anyhow—better now instead of later.*

All these thoughts rolled around in his head. *But I want to keep her!*

Dillon begged Dr. Jenkins to let him go home.

○ඃ৪০

The following Friday afternoon, Angie was getting ready to go to the bus station. *I'm going to have a talk with that Dillon McCandless. He is not to ever talk to me that sharp again.* She was rehearsing what to say.

The doorbell rang and she almost didn't answer it, afraid she'd miss the bus if she got talking to someone.

Opening the door, she gasped at Dillon standing there, crutches under his arms, smiling at her. He dropped his crutches, leaned against the house, grabbed her, kissed her suddenly and whispered over and over "I'm sorry, I'm sorry—don't ever leave me."

"Oh, Dillon. You're foolish. Don't you know how much I love you?" It was the first time she had said 'I love you.' "How did you get here? How did you drive your car?" The worry was back in her voice.

"Nothing to it, Angel. Nothing was going to keep me away." He kissed her again and then picked up his crutches. "Come with me. Get in the car. We have to talk."

Once he was settled back in the driver's seat of his Ford, he accomplished an incredible feat; leveling his crutch in and out on the clutch, he shifted and drove off to Backesto Park.

"Let's just sit here. It's too hard to get in and out." The staring began again. They both got pleasure just looking at each other. "You first," said Dillon. "Say what you want. I deserve any tongue lashing you give me."

Angela began, "Dillon, you are to never again talk so sharp to me. My father has never talked to my mother like that."

"This isn't about your father. What is he? Your knight in shining armor riding on a white horse?" He was annoyed, not liking being compared to Rico.

She snapped back, "He's supposed to be special to me. He's my father!"

"Well, I don't think I can compete with that. You don't really know me. I'm not a very nice guy. I have a temper." His tone changed. "I wish I could be what you want me to be, but I don't know if I can." His pleading sounded desperate. "What I know, is that I need you in my life. You make me feel like a better person and I'll try. I really will try. Just don't leave me."

Angie gave him her best smile and put her hand on his cheek. "You don't have to compete with my father, and I think you're a very nice guy. Let's not talk anymore. Will you just kiss me? I've missed you so much."

There was a moment of awkwardness as he tried to move to her. "You'll have to do the kiss, I can't turn toward you."

She smiled and moved in front of him. As she did, she silently raised a prayer to heaven, *Thank you, God. Now he will have to behave chaste.*

A while later, when it was time for Dillon to drive her back home, he shared, "I won't see you 'til next week or maybe I'll come up Sunday. But tomorrow I have to be at the clinic to have the cast changed. It will take all day."

She could see how tired he was and she was sure he was in pain. "Don't come on Sunday. Wait 'til you're better. Rest up. I'll see you next week.

Chapter 6

Once Dillon had gained most of his strength back, double dating became the norm. Earl Goforth was Dillon's best friend. Their bond was cemented in high school. Whenever they cut class or caused a ruckus, they were put on the grounds patrol together. They proudly took credit for having planted most of the trees at Live Oak High.

Vivian Fantozzi, a spunky red-head, was Earl's girlfriend. Dillon had once taken her out to the Big Orange hot dog stand, but she had eyes only for Earl.

The three of them grew up together and became friends for life. Like Dillon, Earl talked very little. He was taller than Dillon, but his main appeal was his sexy eyes that were kept at half-mast most of the time. He was poor, like Dillon, so they took jobs at the local mushroom plant, going into the darkened growing rooms, and wearing the lanterns on their foreheads to harvest the mushrooms. They hated the job, but needed the money.

Vivi, being Italian, often invited them over for dinner. Her mother, Pia Fantozzi, loved to feed them, always saying she would fatten them up, knowing how poorly they ate.

Once Angie joined the group, the four of them went out every Saturday night. They would drive around downtown San Jose in Earl's '41 Ford coupe, cruising the main streets, and checking out the other cars.

Sometimes they drove back to Morgan Hill. There was Tacci's Drive-In Restaurant next to the Texaco gas station, and across the road was the "Gray Sheet" motel. If the boys had just gotten paid, they would go to Tacci's to eat his specialty, spaghetti and meatballs. Afterwards, it was back to San Jose to the drive-in theater.

Often the girls would climb into the trunk, so they only had to pay for two tickets. They only got caught once as they were climbing out.

Dillon had switched from brandy to beer and always brought a six-pack, sometimes two, just for himself, since Earl, Vivi, and Angie didn't drink alcohol. Months passed and the four of them grew even closer together.

Photos courtesy of Carol Tacci

The school year was coming to an end and Angela had been voted one of the princesses for the Senior Ball. Even though he couldn't dance, Dillon promised to take her. Her prom dress had tiers of pink fluff. Not allowed to wear strapless dresses, Angie fashioned some pink tulle around her shoulders, so it would pass inspection from the principal.

Angela wasn't looking forward to the dance, knowing how uncomfortable and self-conscience Dillon would be with a cast and crutches. They had gone to the Christmas Dance and it was a disaster. Dillon was grumpy all night so after the picture was taken, they left early. But this was the Senior Ball: the last high school dance!

Opening the door, Angie was ready to tell him that they didn't have to go. "Dillon, what have you done?" she shrieked.

"All I've done is get a haircut. Tony, your neighbor, the barber, talked me into it. It's called a crew cut. Don't you like it?"

His shaggy white-blonde locks had been buzzed, very short in Angela's opinion. "I don't know," she answered. "I liked the way it was." She walked around him, looking at him from all sides. "You look different." She was somewhat disappointed, thinking she'd never again see his fair hair blowing in the wind. Actually, he did look pretty cute. She rolled her hand over the spikey hair.

"Forget the hair, what else do you see?" Angela noticed the new one-buttoned blue suit he was wearing and his blue suede shoes. Two of them. No cast! No crutches!

"Oh, Dillon, you look wonderful. Are you okay? Are you in pain? Can you walk?

"Angel, Angel, I'm fine. Doc gave me some good pain pills. Don't think we'll be dancing, but at least I'll look normal." He grabbed her hand. "Come on, let's go have dinner first. I'm taking you to that fancy Shadow Brook Restaurant where you have to ride a tram down to the entrance." He paused and gazed at her for a few seconds. "You look beautiful. Here's your corsage. Vivi picked it out.

Those are baby pink roses. He helped her open the box and pinned it to the tulle on top of the prom dress up at her shoulder.

"They are so beautiful. Now I'm ready"

Getting into the front seat of his Ford, Angie spotted the six pack of beer on the floor in the back seat. Only three left. She always made excuses for whatever Dillon did. *He must be in an awful lot of pain,* she thought as Dillon slid into the driver's seat. *I'm sure the beer and pills help.*

Most Notre Dame High School dances were held at the San Jose Women's Club, but this year the Senior Ball was being held at the classy Lyndon Hotel in Los Gatos. Once past the bustling line at the entrance to the dance, Dillon and Angie sat together at a corner table watching the dancers, listening to the live band. At different intervals the most popular records of that year were played: "Put Your Head on my Shoulder," "Wake Up, Little Suzie," and more. Everyone loved dancing to "Rock Around the Clock," and doing "The Twist" or "Mashed Potato."

Angie hummed to the songs, glancing at Dillon. She saw how much he hated being there. He had a surly look on his face and she noticed he kept swallowing pills.

Looking around the dance floor, Dillon thought, *I want to punch out every one of these smart-ass Bellarmine boys*. Dillon clenched his fists under the table. *What a bunch of puking pansies! They wouldn't last two hours doing some real work.* "Let's get out of here, Angie. I've had enough."

"Dillon, just a little longer. They're about to take the picture of the queen and princesses."

Once back at the car, Dillon yanked off his suit jacket and tie, grabbed the beer and swallowed more pills. Angie was disappointed to leave early. *At least he took me and we did take our picture as a remembrance.*

Dillon was forgiven again.

(left) Dillon and Angie at the Christmas Ball (right) Angie and Dillon
at the Senior Ball

Angie (second from the right) with Senior Ball Queen and princesses

Graduation was soon approaching them. Practicing for the event, Sister Mary Delarosa stood at the top of the stairs of the church. As each girl came up the steps, she handed out Kleenex to those who had on too much lipstick. She also checked their legs to make sure they

were wearing nylons. Too often, the girls would draw a seam line down the back of their legs with an eyebrow pencil and try to sneak it past the sister's watchful eyes.

Angie was the student body president, always an overachiever. The principal had even cornered her one day in the school halls in order to convince her to join the convent when she graduated because she had heard of her daily mass routine.

Surprised at the suggestion, Angie choked out, "I'll pray about it, Sister," as she thought about her impure acts with Dillon.

Angie (second from left)

The night of graduation, Dillon asked Angie to marry him. He had an engagement ring in his pocket. First he handed her a magnifying glass, then he opened the ring box, revealing a one-fourth carat solitaire.

"Vivi helped me pick it out. It's not very big. Someday, I'll buy you a bigger one."

"Dillon, it's the most beautiful ring I've ever seen. I don't need a bigger one. I'll marry you tomorrow, but first you must ask my father's permission. I'll keep the ring safe and as soon as you get the okay, I'll put it on."

"My God, Angie, I'm not marrying your father. You're a big girl. Just tell me YES!"

"Yes, yes, yes, but first you must ask Papa."

The next day, the graduation party was held in the Divencenzi's backyard. Grape vines grew over the summer-house providing a roof, giving cover to the table. Every now and then, a long green worm dropped from the vines onto the tables.

Serafina had decorated with crepe paper and placed all of Angie's school awards on display. Rico was working outside, tending his strawberry barrel and tomato plants, as usual, dressed in his suit and tie for all occasions

Dillon was still uncomfortable with Rico, but regardless, he marched up to him and blurted out, "I want to marry Angela. Do I have your permission?"

Rico was surprised by the sudden request, but it wasn't unexpected. "Take a walk with me, Dillon." They headed out of the summer-house and over to the bird aviary. Rico had just put last year's Christmas tree inside for the birds to perch on—Angie had told Dillon about the famous Rico Christmas trees. He paid little money for the worst looking Christmas tree on the lot. Once it was home, he began to deconstruct it, removing all the branches. He drilled holes in the trunk and put a glob of chewing gum inside each hole. He then re-inserted the branches until it was rounded out to a perfect shape. After the Christmas season, the tree would be left outside to dry a bit and then it became a new perch for the aviary. Dillon was fascinated to see several dozen yellow canaries, fly, flutter and warble as Rico approached them.

Rico began to change their water and fill the seed holders, not saying anything for a full five minutes. Dillon stood beside him, shifting his weight from side to side until, finally, Rico spoke. "What do you do for a living, Dillon?"

"I drive a cement mixer. I'm in the Teamsters' Union and make pretty good money."

"How much school did you have?"

"I dropped out of high school my senior year to help pay all the hospital bills my father had for my mother."

"Well, that's honorable, but education is important."

Getting annoyed, Dillon thought, *I don't want, or need, a lecture.* "Listen up Rico," he said, rudely emphasizing his first name. "I'm going to marry Angela, with or without your permission. I love her and will always take good care of her and she loves me too. This was her idea for me to ask permission. She just wants you to approve."

Rico looked away from the birds and directly at Dillon, noticing his chin raised, thumbs stuck in the Levi's pockets, daring him to say no. He liked his spunk, but still… "Tell you what, Dillon. I want Angela to have a little more schooling. I want her to go to College of Notre Dame in Belmont. You can still see her on the weekends. One year of school, then we will plan the wedding."

Dillon walked away. *How in God's name can I last one year without having her.*

❁

Come late August, it was time to drive Angela up to Belmont. She had to carry her own suitcases into the building, as no man was allowed to enter the dormitory. Dillon felt like he was sending her away forever.

"If you want, come up on Wednesdays. I can see you for two hours, from 3:00 to 5:00. Then, on Friday, I'll get on the 4:00 train home. We can have the whole weekend together and you can drive me back on Sunday night."

College of Notre Dame was a small, all girls, campus. The buildings were set high in the Western hills, situated on the majestic, Ralston Estate. Every evening, dinner was served in the mansion, with its floor to ceiling mirrors gracing the huge ballroom. Angie helped with the tuition by setting and unsetting the dinner tables. At dinner, the girls were expected to dress formally every night and to participate in the planned topic of discussion; a card placed on each table, outlining the dinner's conversation. The first night's suggested talk was the upcoming Eisenhower election.

Angie shared a room with Jacqueline, a beauty of a girl and worldlier than Angie. They were compatible roommates, as long as Angie covered for her by letting her back into their bedroom through the window. Jacqueline regularly slipped out the window to meet her boyfriend.

Jacqueline never seemed to study. Two days before exams she would take no-dose tablets and stay up all night studying. She always managed to get A's.

Angie had a full load of classes, taking 19 units, and needed to study a minimum of two hours each night. But she didn't mind. She enjoyed the professors that treated the students as adults, encouraging them to ask questions and debate them.

Across the hall was the chapel. There was no daily mass, but Angie relished sitting in the quiet room, reading or writing a letter to Dillon.

She also learned to smoke, up on the roof top room, bringing a half pack of Viceroys from home each week. Papa never missed them.

It was a two hour drive one way from Morgan Hill to Belmont. Dillon was burning the tires off his car going back and forth. On Wednesdays, they mostly sat in the parking lot and just talked for the allotted two hours.

She asked him about their mutual friends, Earl and Vivian, and she also asked him to explain how he came to be friends with that horrible Orville from the night they met. "He was never really my friend. We were at the fair together because we had entered our hogs in the agriculture section. A lot of politics goes into who gets the blue ribbons. I had the best hogs; anyone could see that, but I got no ribbon." He sounded bitter as he guzzled down the last of his beer and popped open another.

Then it was time for a quick, passionate kiss.

"I love you, Angel."

"I love you too, Dillon."

 At the end of each one of their meetings, she raced up the hill to Ralston Mansion, so she wasn't late for her job of setting tables for dinner.

They didn't double date as much anymore. Dillon wanted to see her alone. The weekends were more tense than enjoyable. The kissing, caressing, and petting were getting more involved, but just short of complete consummation. Angie managed to halt the progress before it got that far.

"You're making me crazy every time you say 'Stop, Dillon.' I don't know if I can wait a whole year, Angel. I want you so much"

Chapter 7

1957

Come vacation, Angie talked to her parents. Not asking them, but rather, telling them, that she and Dillon wanted to get married in January. She had just turned 18. Dillon was 22.

Why the rush? Eda thought; she worried that Angie might be pregnant, but she said nothing. Rico also said nothing, secretly glad that he wouldn't have to keep paying the expensive tuition.

The very next day Eda and Angie went out and shopped for a wedding gown. She chose a gown that resembled her senior ball dress, with fluffy tiers on the side but with long lace sleeves and a long lace train. Serafina, Caroline Childrey—a friend from school, and Laetitia needed dresses too, as they would make up the bridal party. Since it was winter, they were to wear two-tone turquoise blue dresses of satin and velvet and they would carry peach flowers. Little Laetitia would be dressed all in peach.

The family ordered the invitations and made announcements for the reception. Everything was accomplished quickly with the wedding a little over a month away.

That night, while having dinner with his father, Dillon brought up the subject of the wedding.

"Do you love her, son— really love her?"

"Yeah, Pop, I really love her. She makes me feel like I'm someone special, like I'm not such a bad guy."

Jacob looked hard at his son and for the first time saw his insecurities. "Since your mother died, you've always been the most important and special person in my life. Do you know that Dillon?" He didn't wait for him to answer. "I want you to be happy."

"I know, Pop. I will be. She's different than any other girl I know. I want to be with her every minute. I love looking at her."

"That's good son. Nothing's better than being with a good woman and Angela is worth looking at."

That was the most personal conversation they had ever shared.

Once they were finished, Jacob spoke again. "You know, Dillon, I can't come to your wedding. Besides, with this junk I wear," he paused, pointing to the oxygen tank he dragged around, "I don't fit in. There will be some mighty important people there. But I'll be thinking of you all day."

"That's okay, Pop. I wish I didn't have to be there either. Angela and I will stop by afterward on our way out of town."

෴

Dillon and Angela went to their appointment with the parish priest. They would be married at St. Patrick's Church, where Angela had attended grade school. They needed a large church to accommodate all the people that would be attending.

The church had an ancient appearance with tall spires and trees growing beside it. The interior had an elaborate gothic altar with various statues bordering it.

Father John Duryea, the priest that would marry them, interviewed Dillon. "Do you promise to raise your children Catholic?" A special dispensation was needed since he was not baptized. The church frowned on mixed marriages, stressing that to have a happy marriage, you should be equally yoked. Because Dillon wasn't baptized, they could not have a Mass with the wedding and they would have to be married outside the communion rail instead of up at the altar.

Realizing how uncomfortable Dillon was, Father Duryea said something about the church being like a ship on the ocean with its rules going this way and that, always sailing toward the horizon. Dillon didn't know what the hell he was talking about, but he appreciated his kindness.

Angela was mentally planning how she would baptize him while he slept. She couldn't bear the thought that if he died, he would be forever in Limbo, a place somewhere between Heaven and Hell.

CঅƸO

Two days before the wedding, Angie took her final exams for the semester, packed up all her belongings, and said goodbye to her friends at College of Notre Dame.

That night at the rehearsal dinner, Dillon told her he would not kneel down at the wedding.

Angie just smiled at him sweetly. "We'll see."

"No more of that that 'we'll see' stuff. I absolutely won't kneel down, Angel. It's your church, not mine." He stated again, emphatically, "No kneeling down. Got that?"

Angie smiled again. "We'll see."

The wedding day arrived with chaos and confusion, complete bedlam. Laetitia couldn't find her bouquet. When she did find it, the dog had chewed half of it. Relatives kept arriving at the house to offer early congratulations and get a preview of the flowing wedding dress they had heard about. Everyone was

Caroline, Serafina, Laetitia, Rico, and Angie

scrambling to get into cars for the drive to the church.

Suddenly, Rico and Angela were alone on the front porch, all the cars had left. They had to get Carmine Bevalacqua to drive them to the church. He leered at Angie as they got out of the car. He sneered, showing his tobacco stained teeth and raising his eyebrows up and down. "Have a nice night, sweetie." Angela got the chills and shivered.

Rico gave him a stern look. "Thanks for the ride Carmine." He then put his arm around Angie protectively, and hurried her into the church

St. Patrick's Church, San Jose

Waiting in the vestibule, Rico gazed intently at his daughter. *When did she grow up?* "You look beautiful, Angela. I want you to have a good life and to take care of your young man. That's your job."

Loretta Wilson

"I will, Papa. Thank you for the wedding."

The music began and they strolled slowly down the long aisle. Serafina, Caroline, and Laetitia preceded them.

Up in front of the altar rail, Dillon was visibly shaking. Every pew in the church was full. *Who are all these people?*

Earl, his best man, patted him on the back. "Buck up ole buddy, it will be over in a few minutes. You're gonna like being married. I do."

Looking down, Earl noticed a blood stain on Dillon's white shirt. "Who stabbed you?"

"Must've cut myself shaving this morning."

"Turn towards me, so no one can see." Earl then took one of his boutonniere pins and pinned Dillon's white jacket over the stain. "Can't have you looking like you've been in a street fight on your wedding day," he laughed as Dillon turned back towards the crowd.

Dillon then saw Angie coming toward him down the aisle. He ex-

haled and stopped shaking. She kissed her father, and came to join him at the altar. She looked like an ethereal being, a celestial angel, his Angel. He couldn't stop staring at her. He reached out to grab her hand. He had to touch her.

Father Duryea cleared his throat twice. Smiling, he whispered, "Dillon, you really have to look at me now."

48

The vows were repeated and then it was time for the final blessing. Angela had mentally rehearsed what she would do. When Dillon held out his arm to walk out, she grabbed hold and pushed and pushed. It was either kneel down or fall down. Down on his knees he went for the final blessing. The wedding was over.

Dillon smiled broadly, walking back down the aisle, showing off his wedding ring that Angela had placed on his right hand by mistake.

The reception was held at the Hawaiian Gardens, a popular and plush place for weddings. The newlyweds stood in the receiving line as the streams of people came up to them offering congratulations. Rico, as councilman, was now taking his turn as mayor of San Jose. Every dignitary in town was there to wish them blessings.

Dillon danced with Eda once while Angela danced with her father. Then they danced together to begin the money dance. Angie wore a cloth bag on her wrist and one by one the men at the wedding came forward and tapped Dillon on the shoulder and put money in her pouch for the privilege of dancing with her and then returned her to Dillon as he waited on the side for the next one to tap his shoulder. This went on for an hour. He hated seeing all those old men dancing with his bride, but he was calculating how much money she was making. *We can have a really nice honeymoon*!

Champagne and hard liquor flowed freely. The meal was scrumptious, lots and lots of food: hors d'oeuvres of salami, various cheeses, smoked salmon, and fruits. The main meal was prime rib, chicken, fish, pasta, many vegetables and, as always, a leafy green salad. The newly married couple walked around handing out traditional Jordan almonds wrapped in netting.

They cut the cake and took pictures until, finally, it was almost time to go.

Laetitia had cake smeared on her face. Her hat was dangling half off. She annoyed people being under the tables, tickling their legs.

Beautiful Serafina was having the time of her life, dancing every dance. She offered to help Angie undress and get ready for the honeymoon. Dillon interrupted her. "I'll help her."

"That a boy, Dillon. You go for it." She winked at him.

Getting Angela out of that wedding gown took forever. Tiny fabric buttons lined the back of the dress from neck to waist. Then she was standing there in a strapless bra and girdle, lacy underpants, garter belt and nylons. Dillon swallowed hard. *Gad-a-mighty*, he thought to himself, never taking the Lord's name in vain, even in his thoughts.

Her going away outfit was a pink, two-piece skirt and blouse with little appliqued flowers. On top of her head sat a pink, pill box hat. Dillon hadn't thought about bringing an extra change of clothes to the church, so he left in his white wedding jacket and black pants.

A few people stood outside and threw rice at them. Most people were still inside eating and drinking, unaware that they were leaving.

Angie kissed her parents goodbye. Thanking them again for the wedding, the two drove off in Dillon's powder blue '52 Ford.

CR&D

They drove south, stopping off to see Dillon's father. He wished them well, kissed Angela, and then they drove on.

Getting as far as Pacific Grove, they stopped at the Wilke's Motel, about one hour south of Morgan Hill. It cost $7.00 per night.

Mr. Wilke noticed the formal white jacket. He watched Dillon proudly sign the registry, Mr. and Mrs. Dillon McCandless. "Seems this is as far south as most brides and grooms get before stopping for the night. Congratulations," he smiled, handing Dillon the key.

Dillon stared at it, hardly believing this was it. Over and over he thought, *at last, at last.* He felt like rubbing his hands together and dancing a jig.

The room was simple, but elegant, with a huge four poster bed with a canopy. Angela had changed into her white, silk night gown and matching peignoir. Dillon stood there, bare chested. He had never owned pajamas and didn't consider buying any now.

Angela stared at him. He had only a few hairs on his chest. A year ago, she had plucked out the first hair she saw and put it in her scrapbook, saying to him "The first chest hair is the first sign of manhood." She had seen him shirtless before, when they went swimming, but this was different. He was all muscle and she thought, *soon I'll be in bed with him, naked.* Her heart started its drum roll. Ta-dum. Ta-dum. Ta-dum. *Oh my.*

"You look beautiful, Angel, but I really want to see all of you. Please, please take off all that stuff."

Slipping the nightclothes off, she quickly jumped into bed and pulled the sheet just up to her waist. She wasn't afraid. On the contrary, she was as excited as he was, anxious to see what would come next after all the caressing and petting.

In seconds he was stuck on her like a fly to honey, each of his words were enunciated clearly, "Don't ever, ever say 'Stop, Dillon' again. All I want you to say is 'Oh, my.' You got that?"

"I promise to never, ever stop you again." That promise was to be kept for 48 years.

Five minutes later, he rolled off of her, staring at the ceiling, breathing hard. His first thought was *Gad-a-mighty.* He exhaled and then softly uttered Angie's favorite words, "Oh, my." Being that it was her first experience, she wasn't too impressed. *So what's the big deal?*

He made love to her two more times that night and once in the morning, each time with a little more finesse, taking his time to give her some pleasure. Slowly, she began to look forward to what he called 'a roll in the sheets."

Early in the morning, while Dillon still slept, Angela slipped out of the bed, ran to the bathroom and returned with a glass of water. Sprinkling a few drops of water on his forehead, she whispered, "I baptize you in the name of the Father, the Son, and Holy Ghost."

Placing the glass on the nightstand, she snuggled up next to Dillon and sighed, *Now, he's right with the Lord.*

Later that morning, they said goodbye to Mr. Wilke and headed south down the scenic Highway 1.

The sun had come out on the wedding day, but now the torrential rains of '57 were back. Highway 1 was washed out in many places making them detour back inland. They couldn't sight see, couldn't even walk on the beach.

"What say you, Angel? Let's just go home?"

"I'd like that. I'm ready to start being a real wife. I'll pack you a lunch and cook you a meal, but just don't expect too much. You know my mother did everything and never taught me a thing!"

He popped another beer and turned the Ford around, heading north to Los Gatos.

CR80

Their first home was a little, one bedroom house. The toilet, with a cracked seat, was in a step-down closet, so their first purchase together was a new toilet seat. The rent was $60 per month.

Dillon went right back to work so that cautious and conservative Angie could save the money from the money dance. From day one they decided that Angie would handle the money since she was the saver and he was the spender. He was more than happy to turn over his paycheck, knowing that his Angel would never say no to anything he wanted to buy. She even saved money in her underwear drawer, but Dillon knew that and often borrowed from it, never putting any back.

She so wanted to be a good wife. She made him bologna sandwiches, putting love notes in his lunch pail. She tried and tried to iron his tee shirts and underwear, then cried and cried when the material wouldn't flatten out. She then just hung a bunch of clothes on the backs of the kitchen chairs, hoping to show Dillon how hard she had worked. She thanked God that his company provided laundered work shirts.

The first week, they ate out so Angie could organize her kitchen with all the wedding presents they had received. She then went grocery shopping, stocking up on foods she thought she might need for meals.

Next came the testing of her cooking skills. Her first dinner was spaghetti. How could she go wrong with that? Open the box and boil the noodles. She remembered seeing her mother simmer the sauce for hours. Using her new iron skillet, the cans of tomatoes simmered until the sauce was gooey. The spaghetti was over cooked and mushy. She stood watching and waiting for Dillon's compliments. With the first bite, he choked, got up from the table and dumped it into the garbage. *How could he do that?* She wondered. *Doesn't he know how many hours I worked at this dinner?* Angie was crushed.

Then she got mad. He was sitting, watching TV, drinking his beer, not caring that her feelings were hurt. "Why are you being so mean, Dillon McCandless? I'm trying. I'm really trying."

He said nothing. She would learn that he always avoided confrontations. There was no apology. Hoping to get a reaction out of him, she shouted, "If you won't even talk to me, then I'm leaving."

He kept watching his program and said nothing.

Out she stomped, not planning ahead what she would do next. Walking around the house she squatted down beside the bushes and peeked in through the window. There he sat, unconcerned about her leaving. *Surely he'll come looking for me after his program*, she told herself.

Another pop of a beer, and another program started.

Angie sat on the ground and cried. It was dark out and getting cold. *Why didn't I bring a sweater? Why did I even get married to him?*

Dillon finally decided to play her game and thought he better go look for her. *She couldn't have gotten too far walking.*

As soon as he drove off, she raced back in, took a hot shower and jumped in bed.

They both preferred to sleep naked. She snuggled down under the blankets and waited for him to return. Three hours later, he finally came home. He said nothing for quite some time, just stared at her with his hands on his hips. She could tell he'd been drinking, but he also looked so tired.

"I went everywhere, Angel. Even across town to your parents' house. I could see through the window you weren't there. Then I just drove all over town looking for you. Is this our first fight? I hope it's our last."

Angie jumped out of bed and ran into his arms. They made love the rest of the night. He was already forgiven.

The nightly ritual always began with Dillon climbing into bed with his back to Angie. He drew his legs up. Angie hunkered down on her side behind him. With her one arm over her head, she'd idly stroked his silky hair. Her other arm snaked under his and she brought it up to his mouth. He placed three quick kisses on her fingertips and she kissed him on his back. Then, like a child fingering the satin binding of a blanket, her fingers began to twine the hair on his chest.

Most nights this began their love play, but on some nights, when Dillon was especially tired, he gently slapped her palm flat on his chest; the signal to just go to sleep. Throughout the night, they turned in tandem. She clung to his back and then the roll over, where she sat on his lap, always naked, with their arms around each other. He held one of her breasts. A compulsion: they had to be touching, touching, always touching.

Chapter 8

1959-1964

Try as you might, you can't slow down Father Time. Two years passed swiftly before Angie was pregnant. She placed a cigar next to Dillon's dinner plate to make her announcement. He agreed to go to classes with her for natural childbirth. At the first session he promptly began hyperventilating during the movie they showed.

Ten months after baby Julie was born, Angie placed another cigar next to Dillon's plate. Then came little Jill, a preemie, only four pounds; Dillon was afraid to touch her, because she looked so fragile.

Ten months later, Dillon watched as Angie laid down another cigar next to his plate. He put his head on the table and groaned; James was born with a full head of dark brown hair. The two girls had light blond hair like their father's.

Dillon looked closely at his son. "Are you sure he's mine?" he joked. After the dark hair fell out, he was bald for a long time; then the little fuzz of white blonde hair appeared. He also had Dillon's magical eyes.

Occasionally, Dillon babysat the kids while Angie had to shop, but he never changed a diaper. If Jimmy crapped his pants, he would put him in the car, hold him down in the front seat with one hand, and drive across town to Grandma Eda so she could change him.

"Angel, we really have to find out what's causing this," he said one day, referencing their quickly expanding family. They both knew, and they both laughed. "Time for me to get snipped." Besides that,

Dillon had several more surgeries on his leg, some reconstructing and then taking the pins out.

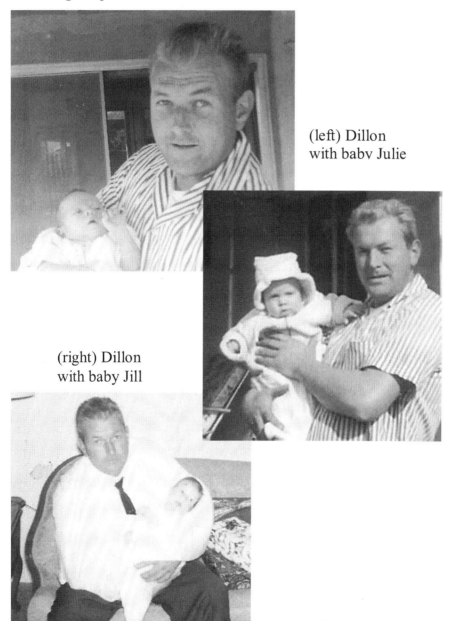

(left) Dillon
with baby Julie

(right) Dillon
with baby Jill

(left) Dillon with
baby Jim

(right) Four-pound, baby Jill. "Too small to hold," said Dillon.

(left) Dillon holding Jill and Julie

Julie, Jill, and Jimmy

Eda and Rico had moved out of their old house and now lived up in the east foothills behind San Jose Country Club. Eda could not part with the 16th Street house that her children were raised in, so they offered it to Dillon, Angie and the kids to live in until they could buy their own house. Angie enjoyed being back in the old neighborhood but she was anxious to settle into their own place.

While Dillon was in the hospital waiting for his leg to heal, Rico took Angela to a house auction on the west side of San Jose. There were two blocks of empty houses that would be auctioned off and moved out to make way for the Valley Fair shopping center. Angie carefully inspected each house until she found the one that would be just right for her family.

"If you really are satisfied with this one, you better bid a little higher." Rico's recommendation was $4,000.

Standing in front of the houses was a couple sadly watching the house that they had built being auctioned off. Instinctively, Angie went up to them. "If I get the highest bid, I want you to know that a young family with three small children will make it a happy home." Her bid was accepted.

That night, dancing with excitement, she rushed to the hospital. "Guess what? I bought a house today. You have 30 days to move it somewhere. Wait 'til you see it, Dillon. It's so perfect."

He was dumbstruck. "What a gal I married! You could run this country if you set your mind to it." Then he got a concerned look. "Where'd you get the money?"

"You know what a saver I am. I've been saving for a house since the day we married, and I didn't save it all in my underwear drawer where you could find it." She was hugging him and laughing. "Do you think your Pop will sell us a couple of acres? We have enough for the house and Papa will make us a loan for the land and the movers. With interest, of course."

"Angel, get the doctors to release me. We have work to do." He was ecstatic to be moving back to Morgan Hill.

CR80

They bought two acres from Jacob that ran west from Monterey Highway to Jacob's remaining 18 acres. They set forms down a long driveway to the house site. Whenever Dillon had leftover concrete in his mixer, he dumped it there. He taught Angie how to begin to smooth it out until he brought his truck back to work and hurried home to finish the troweling.

After the piers were set down, they were ready for the house. It was cut in half and in the middle of the night, it slowly made its way down Monterey Highway 25 miles south to Morgan Hill. They picked the perfect site for the house: right next to a huge oak tree. Their family would be neighbors to Jacob. Dillon was so relieved to be able to look in on him, and made it a habit of visiting him every day after work.

Angie promised to walk a meal over every night. Her cooking skills had improved and she tried to encourage Jacob to eat more. He had emphysema and dragged his oxygen tank with him wherever he went. The only time he was without it was when he would turn off the oxygen and walk outside, where he would begin to roll a cigarette, always carrying the tobacco pouch and papers in his shirt pocket. Old habits were hard to break. When he ran out of tobacco, he would walk, ever so slowly, taking two steps, bending over with his hands on his thighs to breathe a bit. Eventually, he'd get to their back door and wheeze out, "Do you have an extra cig?" Angie always gave it to him without a lecture. Then she'd drive him home.

He had two joys in life: rolling his cigarettes and watching Dillon's three little kids running around his house, playing in his empty chicken coup, laughing when they came out with their legs covered in black fleas and turning the hose on them to wash the fleas off.

Angie knew he was lonely, so she often went over during the day. She grew to love her father-in-law and was fascinated by the stories he told of his young life in Edinburgh, Scotland. Then came the stories of life in the U.S. Navy, followed by a drunken spree that led him to enlist in the Canadian Army during WWI, and finally coming home to Kearney, New Jersey to marry the girl next door.

Angie would quickly run home afterward to write down his stories. *Someday, I'm going to write a novel about him.*

One of the first things Angie did when they settled in was register at St. Catherine Church, and put the children into the St. Catherine Parochial School. It was here that Jimmy would learn to be an altar boy. It made Angie so proud to see her son serving at mass. Dillon worried they might turn him into a priest.

Every Sunday, they dressed in their best clothes to attend mass. Dillon would stand on the porch to wave them off or walk them to the car. During the mass, Angie whispered to each child to pray and offer their communion for their father. She would sometimes look around and see whole families sitting together and feel a pang of envy.

Angie, Julie, Jim and Jill going to Easter Sunday Mass

At first, she wasn't too thrilled about the town of Morgan Hill. Telfer's was the main grocery store. Three miles to the south was Rocca's and five miles to the north was Mike Bonfante's Madrone Market. Closer to their house, in San Martin, was a smaller grocery store, Jack's Market. It was not run by Jack, who worked in San Francisco, but by his wife, Vita Lo Monaco and their two daughters, Johanna and Rosemarie.

Down town there was Robert's Department Store which carried a limited selection of items, and The El Toro, run by Al Leonetti, which catered to men's clothing and shoes. Al always kept one box of slippers in the back room just for Dillon. He knew that sooner or later, Dillon would come in to buy them; no one else would.

"Hey, Al, it's time for me to buy another pair."

"You got it Dillon. Been saving these just for you." Al went to the back room, blew the dust off the box and presented it to him.

During the day, Dillon only wore cowboy boots, but after hours, he wore those high top, brown, leather "old-man" slippers.

For entertainment, there was the Granada Theater showing outdated movies.

Regardless of the inconveniences, Angie soon came to love the charming town, surrounded by hills: the perfect place to raise children.

Moving the house

Angie troweling the concrete

The finished project, home in Morgan Hill

Chapter 9

Eda often came for a visit. Dillon could tell how long it would be by the number of suitcases she brought.

Upon one arrival, she cornered Angie and told her she had come to improve her domestic skills. From one small satchel she brought out the jars of her magic formula for doing laundry: Borax, bluing, bleach, baking soda, vinegar and other unidentified bottles. She then attacked the linen closet; everything came out: sheets, pillowcases, towels, table cloths.

"Your clothes have the gray sickness," she stated. The washing machine rotated for hours.

Eda complained to Dillon, "When are you going to put up some clothes lines?"

"Eda, Angie has a brand new dryer."

"A dryer is what's wrong. They turn the clothes gray." She then proceeded to drape the wet clothes on the bushes and spread the sheets on the lawn in front of the house. "Clothes need sunshine to get white."

Angie pleaded with Dillon to have patience with Mama. "She means well."

Eda's next attack was in the back yard. Dillon held his tongue as she went to war with the garden, but prayed she would leave before she did any damage to it.

Dillon and Serafina had always gotten along. They drank beer to-gether and she'd tell him shady jokes. She had also given him some special high grade seeds to plant. He soon had a row of marijuana growing about 18 inches tall.

During her tirade, Eda found a hoe in the garage. "Just look at all the weeds!" Whack. Whack. Whack. And with that, Dillon's prized crop was gone. Angie and Dillon often wondered if she had known what it was.

The children had many pets; three of them were tortoises: Snort, Flash, and Bambi. In the winter they were placed in shallow boxes until they woke up in the springtime. From November to March, they slept, never moving an inch. Those boxes were kept under the bed where Eda slept when she came to visit. Next to the tortoises was a portable keyboard that Angie took to the retirement home to play songs for the elderly.

It came time for the tortoises to wake up right as Eda lay down after a long day of her instructions to Angie. Crawling out of their shallow boxes and across the keyboard, the tortoises flicked up the "ON" button on the keyboard and began to make music as they slowly walked over the keys. Eda leapt out of bed, got dressed quickly, and stuffed all her clothes in her suit case, exclaiming, "I'm going home! This is a crazy house."

Dillon loved Eda, but as he placed the tortoises outside in their pens, he thanked them for cutting her visit short.

CS&O

Dillon much preferred when he got to see Angie's sisters. Beautiful Serafina, raising two children on her own, was divorced and still single. She dated a variety of men. There was the one who wore a faucet on a chain around his neck. He claimed that his thoughts could now flow freely. Dillon avoided him like the plague every time Serafina came to visit.

Chuck was another one. He was one of her favorites. She adored his raspy voice. He was an ex-drug addict and a carpet salesman. He no longer did drugs and his carpets were such a deal, that Angie and Dillon bought some from him and he did the installation. They didn't ask where the carpets had come from since the price was right.

Sera liked the bad boys best. One boyfriend took her to the Reagan inauguration in Washington, D.C. He also had listed her on his business papers as the vice president of his company until her lawyer friend advised her to disassociate her name from his company. He was never very clear about what his business was, always just saying that he fixed things!

At her daughter's wedding, there was a table in the corner where all her old boyfriends sat together.

The most normal man that she dated was Jerry, a retired sheriff. He had asked her to marry him, just once. She said no. "I love him five days a week, not seven." He never asked her again. As getting to know her, he became afraid that she would spend him into bankruptcy. Jerry loved her for the fun she brought into his life, but he recognized her irresponsible spending habits. She once took her two children to Hawaii and ignored the utility bill for three months until the power was turned off.

Serafina and Jerry

Eda begged her to marry Jerry. The family loved him and hoped he would bring stability to her life. "I can't die peacefully 'til I know you're married and settled down," Eda would argue every time the subject arose.

It just wasn't meant to be, but she dated Jerry for the next fifteen years, until the day he died from a sudden heart attack. He left her a nice chunk of money. Everyone thought Sera was just too much woman for him, but he surely died a happy man.

Eda and Rico were well into their 40s when Laetitia was born. They were neither prepared for nor capable of raising a child of the free love 60s. Laetitia had gone to university for five years and then on to Japan where she continued to study art, the favorite major of the times. Rico would always ask, "When will she get a job?" Years later, she would put all that education to good use and become a successful art teacher at a private school.

But having left the Catholic Church as a young adult, Laetitia embraced various Eastern traditions, always trying to get Rico to get in touch with his emotions. Eda thought the solution to all problems was food. She was ever ready to feed the Woodstock runaways that Laetitia brought home, but whenever Laetitia mentioned expressing feelings, Rico broke out in a sweat. He could not understand what she was talking about. He would attack the situation as a business project. He insisted she accompany him on a weekend retreat, hoping the lectures would inspire her to return to the true faith. The two of them traveled to the novitiate house high in the Saratoga hills.

That first night, a handsome young seminary man, dressed in priestly garb gave the opening prayer. Laetitia took one look, pointed to him and declared to Rico, "I'm going to marry him."

Shocked, Rico blustered helplessly, "Not only do you leave the church, now you plan to take a man of the cloth with you!"

Once back home, Dale, the seminary man, called Laetitia daily. She lied to him, saying she was thinking about coming back to the church. "Maybe you could counsel me and help me find the right path."

After two weeks of phone calls and fictitious counseling sessions, he showed up at the house, neatly dressed, minus the priestly garb. They never really dated. He had no money and no job. Rico tried to talk them into waiting, but Laetitia was adamant. The seminary man simply said, "The Lord will provide, the Lord will provide."

Eda would say, "Does he expect Jesus to come down and pay the bills?" Throwing up her hands in defeat, she began to plan the wedding.

For the reception, Eda chose the magnificent Villa Montalvo, high in the Saratoga hills, since it was near the place where they had first met.

Eda had put her foot down when Laetitia had wanted it to be a potluck. "Everyone can bring their favorite dishes and desserts. Mama, maybe someone will even bring pot brownies, won't that be fun?" Eda wasn't sure if Laetitia was joking, so, breathing deeply, she challenged her, "It will be catered!" She gave in on the ordered wedding cake which Dale had designed: a huge chocolate cake in the shape of the cross.

True to the hippie movement, Laetitia told the bridal party to wear whatever they wanted. Willing to oblige her, they all dressed differently. The girls had on flowered dresses of many colors with fresh flowers in their hair. One groomsman had a green suit, another wore a tuxedo but came barefooted, and one wore jeans and tee shirt.

Spunky Laetitia was delighted with the unconventional look. She and Dale, however, had the traditional garments: suit and white wedding gown. She added a pink sash around the waist just to be contrary. Eda had heart palpitations when she saw their attire.

Dale and Laetitia

Because they got married on Easter Sunday, instead of the traditional Jordan almonds wrapped in net, the newlyweds gave out colored Easter eggs. Old Uncle Joe stared at his egg. He shook his head, "You know, Rico, they're not really married. No Jordan al- monds."

The crushing blow to Eda was that there had been a murder on the grounds of the Villa. She had to give the Police Department a copy of the guest list. This wedding had aged her ten years. She put no article in the Mercury newspaper announcing the wedding.

Chapter 10

1968-1979

Earl and Dillon began building Tote-Goats, a sort of motorcycle with a very long seat. Dillon always said Earl could build anything, just give him a welder. They would use them for hunting, but also for the family outings. Angela, Dillon, Jimmy and Julie rode on one. Earl and Vivian had only one daughter, Tammy, so Jill rode with them.

Tammy and Jill grew up best friends, nearly sisters. Having only one child, Vivi was very protective of her daughter. Tammy would cry to her mom, "You never let me go do the fun things like Jill does."

Vivi would explain to her, "I only have one. If Angie loses a child, she still has a couple of spares. End of discussion!"

Often they trailered the Tote-goats over to the Watsonville beach and then drove on the wet sand along the water's edge. Sometimes, Dillon drove farther into the ocean and managed to get everyone wet and screaming, just for the fun of it. Earl, Vivi, Tammy and Jill followed right behind them.

They dug for clams and roasted hot dogs on open fires. Late in the day they huddled by the fire on the beach to get dry and keep warm and made

Earl, Tammy, and Vivian

s'mores, melted marshmallows and chocolate on graham crackers, for dessert.

Life was good. Those were halcyon days.

Living in the country, most kids had horses to ride. Earl and Vivi had bought Tammy an older but tame mare to ride. Angela and Dillon decided it was time to buy one for Jill. Jimmy liked motorbikes better and Julie liked to read, so Dillon and Earl went horse hunting.

They found a local horse trader known only as Oscar. He assured them that George, the horse they were looking at, was sound, a perfect gentle horse for a young girl. The two men knew little about horses; it had four legs and a tail, looked alright standing-up, so Dillon paid Oscar $50 and trailered George home.

Dillon thought he should try him out before putting Jill on his back, They quickly discovered that George was blind in one eye when Dillon tried to mount on his blind side. He was barely in the saddle when George began to roll his eyes crazily, snorting and bucking. Dillon went flying, landing in the dirt, calling out to Earl, who went chasing after the horse. "Just bring the saddle back." They never saw George again.

Dillon got better advice for the next purchase. Gretchen was an older bay mare, similar to Tammy's.

Come Fourth of July, the two girls and Cousin Laura rode in the parade bare backed, dressed in itchy burlap sack dresses that Angie had made along with moccasins

and feathers in their hair like Indians.

The girls would have horses until they were married and left home.

Dillon and Earl often went on hunting and fishing trips together, usually up near Lake Tahoe, Nevada. Always a loyal and understanding friend, Earl never criticized Dillon about his drinking. He did his best to keep him out of trouble. Earl never drank alcohol. He was a Coca-Cola man with only one vice: the three packs a day he smoked.

Dillon finally decided to turn in his old '52 Ford for something new. It had too many miles on it, but still it was difficult to part with. Another old friend, Bruno Gamez, went with him to the Ford dealership. He helped Dillon pick out a new Ford pickup and bought a used jeep to tow behind for hunting. He bought Angie a classy LTD Town and Country station wagon that would accommodate their growing family.

CꙄꙄ

The City of Morgan Hill sponsored a Junior Rodeo, so Dillon and Jimmy decided to check it out. The prizes were on display and Jimmy was eyeing the lariat. "I'd sure like to have that rope," he told his dad.

"Son, you go for it. How hard can it be to chase down a calf?"

Jimmy signed up for the Calf Scramble and tolerated the taunts and jeers directed at him by the out of town cowboys. "He thinks he can win wearing tennis shoes!"

They stopped laughing at him when he bull dogged the calf in record time running into a wall and getting a bruised face.

Dillon was so proud of him. "I'll buy you a rope. You go claim your first prize." Jimmy would wear that big silver belt buckle for years to come.

When he got a little older, Jimmy went with his dad on the "Big Hunt" every year, in Salmon, Idaho, a little town with friendly people. In Salmon, they stayed at the Owl Inn and mostly ate at the local restaurant. The townsfolk looked forward to the hunters coming to town, hoping they would spend their money to help the economy. Over the years, they would often invite the travelers to dinner at their homes. Angie sent jars of canned pickles and salsa as gifts for them.

Dillon could not walk the hills, so he just drove the jeep and drank his beer, letting Jimmy do all the leg and lifting work.

They made some deer jerky, but the meat was mostly given to the locals. Angie tried making different recipes with the venison, but they never acquired a taste for the wild meat. The hunting trip was more about spending time together, father and son, then it was about getting the biggest buck.

ॐ

Boats, lakes, and especially the ocean always played a big role in the family's outings. When the children were very little, their first boat was aluminum, not much bigger than a row boat, with a 25 horsepower motor. Putting life jackets on the kids, Dillon and Angie never considered any danger going out through the Moss Landing harbor into the open ocean. The kids squealed with delight as the little boat bobbed over the waves and they all got soaking wet as a larger boat caused a deep wake that sprayed them.

Several years later, Dillon thought he might like to learn how to sail. He and Angie took a three hours lesson out in the San Francisco Bay. They bought a sailboat named Elijah and prepared for their first voyage with the kids.

Jimmy never had his father's love for the ocean but he enjoyed going places with his dad and he hoped that maybe this time he wouldn't get sea sick.

They hoisted the sails and managed to not hit the rocks going through the harbor. After several hours, Dillon decided that sailing really was too much work. Coming back in, Jimmy was turning green and puking over the side of the boat. Wanting the day to be over, he lowered the sails too soon. The boat had no power and, as they headed for the dock, Dillon hollered out, "Angie, throw your body in between the boat and the dock, so we don't scratch it!"

Seeing her expression, he started laughing as they crashed into the dock. "Only kidding, Angel, only kidding."

That very afternoon the Elijah was traded in for a larger fishing boat which was kept moored in the harbor.

৩৪৪৩

Dillon received five weeks paid vacation each year, so they carefully planned each trip. In summer, they would camp at various lakes.

Dillon would set up the tents, cots, and butane stove. Angie laid out the oil table clothes, put out the lanterns, and set up the makeshift kitchen. One of Dillon's many boats would be docked at the campsite, ready for the kids to water ski all day. Then came the barbeque dinners and campfires at night.

In the winter, the kids were dropped off at the snow ski resorts, while Dillon and Angie went to the casinos. Jimmy especially was an avid skier, always selecting the steepest slopes. "Gun Barrel Run," was his favorite.

On one such trip, driving to the ski area, the weather had turned cold and snowy; consequently, chains were required for the car's tires. Dillon had never had a problem with spending money, but for some reason, paying $20 to the chain gang standing along the road was an insult to his manliness. "It's a simple job. I can do it in a few minutes," he said determined to put on the tire chains himself.

Angie appreciated his effort to save money, something he rarely did, so she praised and thanked him for being so thrifty.

Somehow, he managed to tangle the chain up under the car. He tugged and jerked, but they held fast. Muttering to himself, he got out a tarp from the trunk and laid it on the ground. Just as he was about to slide under the car, a truck passed by, covering him with snow and slush.

After that, he was happy to pay the chain gang to unhook the chains and put them on the tires.

Even when his temper flared, the kids were never afraid of him. On the contrary, they were delighted to hear his colorful expressions of anger. It made them hunker down in the back seat with their hands over their mouths trying hard not to laugh out loud.

Angie handed him a towel to dry off as he climbed back into the car, thanking him for trying, and doing her best to calm him down.

⋛⋚

Most vacations were memorable, happy times. One, however, no one would ever forget.

Dillon had insisted that the children needed to see Mount Rushmore. After driving ten hours on the first day, they were all tired and hungry. The family stopped at a place that they weren't sure was a house or a café. A young man wearing an apron was sitting on the front porch, his feet up on the front railing. The sign just said "Open."

As they got out of the car, he jumped up and ushered them in. They must have been his first and only customers of the day. He kept saying, "Welcome, welcome," as he held the door open for them.

There was no menu, but he assured them that he had just made a delicious meatloaf with rice and beans that very morning. He brushed the dust off the table and said, "I'll get started with your meal as quick as I can, just have to wash up some dishes and silverware. You folks just relax."

Angie and Dillon exchanged looks, but they were too tired to get up and go somewhere else, besides, it was a good two hour drive to the next town.

The meal was passable. They used the not too clean restroom, paid the bill, and left to find a motel. Within a half hour, the whole family had cramped up and had diarrhea. One of the kids had an accident, making the whole car smell like an outhouse. Then, with his belbelly aching, Dillon had to get out and change a flat tire

The trip was only to get worse. As they continued to leave the main road over and over to find a rest stop, they ran out of gas. Luckily, they carried an extra five gallons of gas and hoped it would get them to a station.

The next kid that needed a bathroom break got the flaring temper instead. "Shit your pants. I'm not stopping again. Gad-a-mighty, the next car we own will have a hole in the floorboards. I'm driving all night to get us home."

Angie lay down in the back seat, and all three children curled up behind the seat in the back of the station wagon. They could hear Dillon grumbling to himself. "My ass is like an overripe tomato splitting a seam."

Angie came awake to ask him, "Just what's that supposed to mean?"

"Angel, do I have to explain everything to you?" She blinked at him, waiting for an answer. He let out an impatient sigh. "Know what happens when it rains on cherries?" Not waiting for her response, "They crack—now do you know how my ass feels? Do you get the picture?"

She was quiet for a second. "How do you think of such things?" she marveled, looking at him with wonder and love. *Only Dillon would use agricultural similes to describe diarrhea*, she thought as she lay back down and slept the rest of the drive home. Mount Rushmore would still be there on their next historical trips.

Another mandatory vacation that Angie would rather forget was paid for by Rico and Eda. All their girls and their families were expected to go to San Jose Family Camp called Camp Tuolumne. Dillon hated organized vacations and really hated camp rules.

There was a time during the day called "quiet hour." Naturally, that was the time of day he wanted to swim. Dillon and the kids were splashing around, enjoying the horse play and making too much noise, when the camp director came running out. She was a husky, tough looking woman wearing a tee shirt and shorts. She stopped in front of them, hands on her hefty hips. Her whistle was shrill and she kept blowing it, motioning them to get out of the water. As they exited the pool, Dillon motioned back to her with a third finger hand wave.

That's all it took to flare his temper. "Pack up the kids, Angel, we aren't staying here another minute."

Angela made her apology to her parents saying Dillon wasn't feeling well. Always dutiful, lest Dillon cause a scene, she loaded up the kids, the clothes, and the camping equipment, and all five of them piled in the station wagon.

They left Camp Tuolumne with Dillon blasting the car horn all the way out during quiet hours

Dillon and a few
of his many boats

Chapter 11

Dillon drove a cement mixer for Western Gravel Concrete Company. He liked his job well enough and got along with the other beer drinking men, but he was always glad to see Friday roll around, so he could be home for the weekend. Once a month, his boss had a safety meeting. Corning ware was raffled off and Dillon always asked Angie what she wanted him to bring home. Almost every month he won a piece of Corning for her.

Cheese and crackers and all the booze you could drink were provided while someone talked about safety. Dillon took advantage of the free beer and usually came home totally crocked, but Angie ignored it, glad he was having fun with the men he worked with and glad to have a new casserole dish.

One of the few times she became angry at his drinking was when he, coming home late at night, began undressing as he got out of the car, got a pillow and blanket out of the trunk, spread it out on the front lawn, lay down and went to sleep there. Angie was worried sick when he didn't come home—until she looked out the front window early the next morning to see him sprawled, buck naked, still sleeping, on the front lawn. *I should just leave him there*, she though. *Let his father or anyone else passing by see him or maybe I'll just turn the sprinklers on him.*

But, of course, she didn't; instead, she shook him awake and hustled him, still naked, into the shower. He was grinning at her with a half-smile, "Come on in, Angel. Let's do a little dancing."

Ordinarily, she would have jumped right in, but this time he had to understand how worried she had been. Putting some anger in her voice, "You can forget that, Mr. McCandless, go to work." Six a.m. she shoved him out the door. Amazingly, he never seemed to have a hangover.

His drinking was escalating. The liquor store was two doors down from his work place, so every Friday night he brought home three cases of beer for the weekend and began drinking them as soon as he got in his car. Steinbrau was his favorite beer. It was cheap and often went on sale. Taking Angie's station wagon, he once brought home 50 cases. "It's such a deal—30% discount."

"That's nice, dear." Angie, the saver, loved a bargain. Being the perfect enabler, she helped stack the cases in an empty closet. During the winter months, when work was slow, she always made sure there was a cold six pack in the fridge every night.

At the next monthly safety meeting, a policeman followed him home and into the driveway. Talking to him, he recognized how intoxicated Dillon was; however, since he was in front of his house, he considered allowing him to just go inside without issuing a ticket. As usual, Dillon mouthed off, calling the cop every vulgar name he knew.

He was jailed for the night. His boss, a friend of the Chief of Police, paid his fine and paid to have it removed from the record and Angie went to pick him up.

Dillon wasn't the only one, who had a brush with the law. Between Dillon's hospital trips, Angie would occasionally have dinner with her Ya-Ya friends, the girls she had gone to school with. They enjoyed getting together, laughing, and bringing their family news up to date.

Coming home late at night from one such dinner, a cop followed Angie right into the driveway. Using his bullhorn, he shouted, "Get out of the car. Get out of the car." It scared her so much that in her hurry to obey the policeman, she tumbled out of the car onto the driveway.

In seconds the cop was over her, shining his flashlight in her face. Terrified, Angie screamed for Dillon to come help her. He heard her calling his name, but in a sound sleep, he took his time coming to look out the kitchen window. Assessing the scene, he hollered out, "Arrest that woman. She's drunk again."

Angie wanted to shoot him on the spot. This was not a good time to be funny.

Dillon could see Angie puckering her lips and narrowing her eyes, and thought he better get out there. "I'm just kidding officer. She really doesn't ever drink. I'm just kidding around," he said, as he helped Angie up off the sidewalk. "Why were you following her?"

The policeman said Angie had been hitting all the little white reflector bumps down the middle of the road and he suspected she was tipsy.

"Naw, she always drives like that," Dillon told him and assured him again, that she never drinks.

Soon the cop and Dillon were laughing together about women drivers. No ticket was issued, but Angie was not laughing.

The kids, on the other hand, loved Dillon's twisted sense of humor. On Halloween night, after too many kids had come trick-or-treating, he grew tired of getting up to answer the door. Deciding to put an end to it, he put on a frightening monster mask, yanked open the front door and sicced Heidi, their dachshund, on the unsuspecting children standing on their porch. The little dog raced out the front door and chased the screaming children down the street. Jimmy fell on the floor laughing.

"Dillon, you've got to stop teaching the children to be so mean. Those poor little kids, you really scared them." Angie stood there, looking concerned.

Oh Angel, lighten up. We're just having fun." He winked at Jimmy. "Bet those little turkeys won't come back here next year."

Angie didn't laugh. She sometimes felt like she was raising four children.

CR♥O

Tight-fisted Angie continued to save money. Dillon continued to spend, but he had developed a good nose for sniffing out potential real estate investments and Angie trusted his judgment. A large piece of land could be divided into four parcels. They would then be flipped for profit, which Angie would manage.

One such land purchase located on the top of Hecker Pass was called "Done Moving." It had a lovely house on it and the family began cleaning and clearing the weeds, making it ready for the land split. An exceptional profit was made and they moved on to the next investment; that one proved to be a scary venture.

They decided to go for broke. Over 100 acres was bought in the beautiful Uvas Canyon and they began drilling for water, producing only dry hole after dry hole. The worry was unbearable. They had invested all their savings and would lose it all if they could not get a decent well to supply all four parcels. Well witchers were brought in and they tried infrared photography, but still the dry holes continued. On the sixth hole, they drilled over 600 feet deep with no success.

At night when they couldn't sleep from worry, Angela and Dillon rode out to the property to watch the progress. It was heart breaking to see the drilling site, all lit up, with the drill blowing dust 200 feet into the air. They had to make the gut wrenching decision of when to shut down the site and start over somewhere else on the property. They were getting deeper and deeper in debt while watching all Angie's careful savings go down the dry holes.

The driller proved to have a compassionate heart. He liked this ambitious young couple and felt bad watching them go broke, so he made them a deal. "I'll punch holes all over these 100 acres. You pay me nothing more, but when I hit water, you pay me double.

Having no more money, and no other choice, they agreed to the deal with a handshake.

All the next week, it rained heavily. Unable to get his rigs up into the hills, the driller decided to try a spot next to the lower roads. The drilling began and like magic, 300 feet deep produced a doozy of a well, giving up ample water for all four parcels and, as agreed, they paid the driller double.

They recouped their investment in the property and made some profit, though it was not as much as expected. Angie was delighted to put the money back in the bank for the next investment. "Thank you Jesus."

They learned a valuable lesson. Never buy a piece of property without water. Never would they get into the well-drilling business again.

∽∾

Dillon had just bought four new dirt bikes for himself and the kids. Before the sale of the property was closed, they spent the day riding all over the beautiful Uvas Canyon hills. Angie had set up a table next to the car and was making sandwiches.

The three kids finally came back down from the mountain and started eating. "Where's your father?" Angie questioned them when she noticed Dillon was not right behind them.

"He was following us, but he didn't come down."

"Well, ride back up and tell him to come eat," she demanded.

You Take the High Road: A Love Story

Jimmy was up and back in a few minutes, yelling down to his mom and sisters to hurry. "Pop crashed on the top of the hill. He can't move. I think he broke his leg.

Angie drove the station wagon up the hill as far as she could. They then made a makeshift litter from blankets from the trunk and they carried him down to the car. Angie knew he had been drinking and was none too gentle getting him back in the wagon, especially when he said, "I didn't want to scratch the bike, so I just laid it down as I skidded. My leg slipped under it." Driving to the hospital, she hit every bump she could.

At the hospital, they said he would have to stay the night. He was too intoxicated to take into surgery.

Back in a cast, Dillon was picked up several days later. Taking him home, Angie confronted him about his drinking for the first time. She suggested they go to see a counselor. Feeling guilty, and knowing that he would be out of work for a while, he agreed to go.

Their appointment was late afternoon. The counselor ushered them in, sat across the desk from them and sighed. He was tired of listening to the wives tearfully blaming all their problems on their husbands drinking.

Angie tried to express her concerns. She loved her husband, but their marriage was suffering. She started telling some of Dillon's escapades. The counselor cut her off short. "All day I've listened to the same stories. I've had a school teacher, a doctor's wife—I've even had a prostitute complain about her pimp. They all say the same thing over and over." He sighed again, and after a minute, he looked at Angie. "How often have you threatened to leave?"

She squirmed and lied. "A few times."

Raising his voice, he said, "But you never followed through, did you?"

"No, sir." He was shouting at her and she started to cry.

"Don't threaten if you aren't going to follow through." Loudly he said, "Just leave him." The counselor threw up his hands after hearing how much and how often Dillon drank. He next looked at him.

Throughout the meeting, Dillon had simply been looking around the office, avoiding eye contact with both the counselor and Angie. It wasn't until the man turned to him that he began to pay attention.

"And you! You're a full blown alcoholic and belong in rehab. Only two percent of alcoholics quit on their own."

Dillon had held himself together throughout the entire session until that moment. He couldn't take any more of this "expert's" opinion. He leaped out of his chair, almost falling over with his cast and crutches. He wanted to smack the man silly, telling Angie to leave him, actually shouting at her, making her cry. He sneered at him, "Jacko, you're looking at one of the two percent." He hobbled out.

Angie was so confused. Why was the counselor angry at her? *What have I done?*

She followed Dillon to the car. They were quiet all the way home. When they pulled into the driveway, Dillon turned to her. "I'm going to prove to you that I can quit anytime I want. Don't ever leave me, Angel. Don't ever."

She saw his beautiful eyes watering, and she leaned over and hugged him.

He kept his word. No more beer. He parked two 35 foot boats in the driveway and began sanding them, tinkering with the engines, repainting and then selling them.

The railroad that ran along Monterey Highway was changing out the train tracks. Not letting his cast slow him down, Dillon got Jimmy and a couple of his friends to help him bring home over 1000 railroad ties. He bundled them in sets of 20 to be used for landscaping and sold them, making a good profit that he turned over to Angie. She continued to manage and save the money.

Chapter 12

Angie and Dillon were always so busy working; days just weren't long enough. When Julie, fifteen years old, announced that she wanted to be a missionary, they said, "That's nice dear," and sent her off to a country that they had to look at a map in order to know where she was.

To toughen up the teenage would-be-missionaries, the sponsors of Teen Missions sent them to camp out in the Florida everglades for the first week. Julie's first letter home told of a water moccasin in their water barrel.

Dillon panicked. "Angel, you better go get that daughter. She's too young to be traveling alone all over the world.

Julie spent the rest of the summer on the Island of Dominica. Her next letter was less dramatic than the first. Julie had met great friends, and was having a blast learning to lay bricks to build the church.

She then dropped a bomb on Angie. "I'll probably not be Catholic when I come home. Mom, the protestant music is so different and the talks are so Biblical and interesting. I'll probably join a non-denominational church."

Angie started to cry. "How can she do this? I've spent her whole life teaching her the true faith."

Dillon said, "Are you so sure there is only one way to God? We'll talk about it when she gets home."

Angie knew he was right, but she still felt like a failure. Julie came home in three months wearing only a tee shirt and shorts, sun burned and full of mosquito bites. Her hair was fashioned in corn rows. She had given all her belongings to the children on the island. The missionary experience impacted her spiritual growth for the rest of her life.

Serving

the

LORD

this

Summer

with

Teen Missions Inc.

DOMINICA TEAM

Julie Wilson
830 Encino Dr.
Morgan Hill, CA 95037

PRAY DAILY

for my. .

1. Spiritual Growth
2. Financial Support
3. Missionary Burden
4. Good Health
5. Traveling Safety
6. Team Leaders
7. and the 642 TEENS and 108 team leaders involved with the '75 evangelistic and work teams taking the Gospel around the world. Also remember the staff of Teen Missions in prayer.

After that, Angie thought she should start paying more attention to what the kids were doing. They seemed to be raising themselves. Angie would see them at breakfast and say "See you at dinner." They played all over the hills of their town and could pretty much do whatever they wanted. Jill on her horse, Jimmy on his bike, and Julie with her nose in a book.

Years later Jill told them of how she would hold on to her horses tail and swim across the Uvas dam. And Dillon and Angie hadn't been concerned as to why Jimmy was wearing a piece of rug under his shirt down his back, until they later learned of a five foot high bike ramp he had built out in the field. The rug, "protected him when he fell off the bike," he told them.

Despite the terrifying stories that would come back to their parents eventually, the kids were growing up to be beautiful, smart, independent adolescents, in spite of their lack of parental guidance.

They were taught to respect adults and how to behave in restaurants. As a child, Jimmy seemed to struggle most with the latter. At one family outing, he would not stop picking at his food, fidgeting, wiggling, or kicking the seat. When he kept it up after being told to settle down, Dillon reached across the restaurant table to flick his ear, knocking a big glass of water all over his own dinner. Uh-Oh. No one laughed.

As parents, Dillon and Angie felt that learning how to work was a mandatory part of their children's education. Dillon bought Jimmy a new lawn mower and he was soon in business with several neighborhood lawns to mow. The girls worked at the Dairy Queen or the hot dog stand at the flea market on Saturdays for half a day, leaving them both plenty of fun time.

The children were also taught to always be generous. They were constantly reminded of how good God was to them and to share what they had with others.

At the time, there were many Vietnamese families in the area who had escaped from communism during the Vietnam War. The church sponsored them, placing the families in homes with the parishioners. Angie wanted to do her part and recognized a lesson to be learned by her young adult children: always be charitable. As a family, they shopped for groceries and delivered food baskets to the sponsored families.

The McCandless children were taught to always "extend a helping hand" to those who are struggling. Jimmy took that advice to heart when his friend Harvey needed a place to stay. Harvey's parents had to move away several months before graduation, so Jimmy invited him to come live in the McCandless house, without asking permission.

Early one morning, Angie discovered two big feet sticking out from behind the couch. Jimmy had been letting Harvey in late at night. They raided the refrigerator and then Harvey went to sleep behind the couch. The two of them would leave for school early the next morning before anyone else was awake.

Surprised, Angie dragged the big teenager out and told him to go sleep in the spare room, Harvey became part of the family until after graduation. He then enlisted in the army.

ॐ

As the kids grew into their teens, Dillon needed another surgery. This time, it was performed on his ankle, so he was given a walking cast and didn't need crutches.

One day, Angie handed Jimmy a grocery list and asked him to go with his dad to the store to buy a few things. Driving to town, a young hot-shot cut Dillon off sharply, causing him to slam the brakes and painfully banged his ankle. The temper flared and Dillon followed the guy, driving barely six inches from his bumper, intending to call him some choice names when he followed him into a Seven-Eleven parking lot. Before Dillon could maneuver himself out of the car, the 'hot-shot' came up to him and, through the open window, punched Dillon right in the eye.

Jimmy loved hanging out with his dad. Something exciting always happened. He could hardly wait to tell his sisters about Pop's black eye.

ॐ

Dillon began drinking beer and popping pain pills again. After four months of total abstinence from alcohol, he felt he had proven to himself and to Angie that he really could quit whenever he needed or wanted to. Angie wasn't so sure, seeing as the number of beers and pills was escalating quickly.

While indulging in enthusiastic sex, Dillon had his first heart attack. He was 40 years old. In the emergency room, to her embarrassment, Angie could hear the doctor trying hard not to laugh as he told the heart specialist what Dillon had told him. "He said when he was having sex, he fell on the floor and flopped around like a big tuna."

They kept him in the hospital for ten days. Angie and the kids came every day and ate dinner in the hospital cafeteria. He was released with instructions to eat less fatty foods and cut back on his drinking. Angie tried to remind him of the doctor's suggestions, but he brushed it off with, "What do they know? I feel fine."

Because of his leg and ankle injuries, he was not able to go back to driving the cement truck, so he increased his buying and selling whatever he could to supplement the income.

"Did I tell you I love you today?" Dillon said as he sat down in his armchair back home.

"Yes Dillon," Angie answered. "You tell me that every day, but you can always tell me again." She smiled.

"How did I get so lucky to have you and such great kids? Angel, thanks for being my wife."

∞

For the next two years, they opened a little three sided shed to sell flowers on the side of the highway as a way to teach the kids a lesson in business. Every Friday afternoon, Angie picked up carnations from Mr. Tamura, a local flower grower. He charged her fifty cents per dozen. Using the suggested markup price for perishable items, Angie sold them for $1.25 per dozen.

Dillon slowly drove the car up the winding Hecker Pass, while Angie and the kids ran alongside, picking ferns and throwing them in the back of their station wagon. These were the greens that went with the carnations until someone told them they would surely be arrested. Apparently, it was against the law to pick anything in the Mt. Madonna County Park. Angie quickly searched for another source of foliage.

The shed was open for half the day on Friday, Saturday, and Sunday, with Julie, Jill, and one of their classmates, Reesa, taking turns operating the flower shed. The shed stood on the 20 acre ranch next door that belonged to Irving B. Perlitch, a local entrepreneur. The town knew him as I. B. Perch.

He charged them no rent and provided free water with the agreement that when they quit selling flowers or when he sold the property, they would tear down the shed and haul it away. There was only one other stipulation: before he would allow them to use his property and shed, Angie had to have her handwriting analyzed by Charlie Cole, a graphologist.

"Why do you suppose he wants to do that?" Dillon asked Angie.

"I don't know. Maybe he wants to be sure I'm not an axe murderer or a criminal."

The next week, Dillon, couldn't let it go and drove up to the Perlitch house to ask him.

Mr. Perlitch explained his reason. "Your handwriting tells everything about your character. Your wife has good character."

"You bet she does!" Dillon agreed. "You'll never have to worry about Angie. She's honest as the day is long. She knows how to handle money too. She can really stretch a buck."

Mr. Perch then invited Dillon to bring his family to his restaurant. "I'll treat you to dinner. That will clinch our deal on the shed."

Come Saturday night they all got dressed to go out to "The Flying Lady" restaurant. The whole ceiling was covered with large models of old airplanes. Mr. Perch was going from table to table visiting with his patrons. When he got to the McCandless family table, he checked out what they were eating.

Looking directly at Jill, he asked, "Why aren't you having my clam chowder?"

Jill answered, "I don't much like clams, sir."

"Well, you have to try my clams," he responded matter-of-factly as he left to go get Jill some chowder.

Having personally brought over a huge bowl of chowder, he placed it in front of Jill. "These clams are fresh. This chowder you will like. Eat!"

After he walked away, Jill stared at the big bowl. Her eyes started watering. She wrinkled her nose and started gagging. Dillon ate most of it and reminded Jill to be sure to thank Mr. Perlitch, and tell him how good it was.

Knowing how much Angie loved business and how good she was at it, Dillon encouraged her to open a full functioning florist business. Angie got really excited with the idea of running her own business. The flower shed served its purpose, mainly to teach the kids how to work and about business, but without refrigeration, expansion would be limited. It was time to close it up.

Dillon got his friend Earl to help tear down the shed. They would use the lumber to build a workshop at Earl's house.

Wanting to show his appreciation for the use of the shed and free water, Dillon asked Earl to help him build a pump house over Mr. Perlitch's well.

Dillon told Angie his plan. "Let's build a small building for your flower shop up on our front acre by the highway. We can always expand it later. You go for it, Angel, and don't worry if the florist business doesn't make it. We can always rent the building out. Knowing you, this business will take off!"

He marked out the perimeter of the future shop and contacted some of the men he used to work with to help pour the foundation. It was then that he got a visit from two union representatives.

"Mr. McCandless, you've been with the union for a long time. Since this will be a commercial building and very visible on the highway, we were hoping you would have a sign up front saying 'All built by Union workers.'"

Dillon hated being told what to do. He was feeling the pressure. That night, he and Angie discussed the situation. She reminded him how very good the union had been to them. She was right. All his surgeries were entirely paid for and he had a good retirement.

The next week, a union contractor was hired and the union sign went up. The building would cost more than they planned for, but somehow, they would manage. Angie wanted no debt when she started her business. It took most of their savings, but the building was paid for.

The county would only give a permit for a septic tank for one year, forcing them to annex their property to the city so they could connect to the sewer line that ran along the highway. Another unexpected expense, but in the long run, it proved to be a good decision.

Angie knew very little about arranging flowers, so she hired an ex-florist to teach her that part of the business. Together they went to the San Francisco flower mart and bought all the stock they needed to begin. Then they were ready and put up the sign "Open for Business."

The only competition was an elderly lady who had been serving the town's flower needs for years. Angie began planning some new ideas for weddings, funerals, and everyday flowers. Soon, one designer was not enough.

In no time at all, they had seven employees. The kids helped de-thorn roses and washed buckets. Dillon helped with deliveries when he was able. A full-time delivery driver was then added to the staff.

Angie enjoyed doing some of the arrangements and quickly got good at it, but her real passion was running the books, doing the buying and selling, and watching the business grow and prosper. She also enjoyed talking to the customers, helping them make decisions. She would always be a people person.

Angie's favorite employee was Randy Adams. She called one day to ask if she could come into the shop and work for free in the back room. She was bored at home. She had always enjoyed arranging flowers and wanted to improve her skills, offering to buy any flowers she used.

Two more rooms had been added to the building to accommodate the additional designers. Randy was given a section of a work table at the back of the room. She didn't talk much, never waited on a customer, and began poking flowers into vases. Angie would soon see her potential.

After several months Angie began to feel guilty, because Randy was filling the cooler box with beautiful arrangements, but receiving no salary. Angie asked her to come on board as a regular employee.

She worked for eight years and became the best designer and a very best friend to Angie. She also got along great with Dillon and often they shared a beer or two together in the backroom.

Randy eventually left the shop to move back to Rochester, Minnesota. She and her husband, Bob, made trips back to Morgan Hill every two or three years for a visit. Their friendship remained solid.

Every three or four months, Angie held a meeting after hours with all the employees. She had prepared a long list of all the items she wanted to address and rolled the paper up. They playfully teased her by calling out "Hail Caesar" when she began to unroll the scroll. Angie was always reminding them to rotate the flowers to the left and always use the flowers on the left first, so that none were wasted. When they went into the cooler box they would begin to march and chant "to the left, to the left, left, right, left."

Angie loved her employees and they loved her. It was truly a family of friends and a fun place to work. Many of the employees would stay and work there for over twenty years.

Chapter 13

Wanting to know more about the Scripture, Angie began attending a Bible study class. She didn't know at the time, but it would bring a new dimension to their lives. Every time she came home, Dillon asked her, "What did you learn?" She was so enthusiastic about the class that she told him everything she could remember, practically teaching the whole lesson over. Then she would tell him about the fascinating teacher she had. Well known in the community, he was a protestant teaching Catholics the Bible, with the permission of their pastor.

Dillon and Angie had received a Bible with their names engraved on it for their wedding present. It sat on the nightstand next to the bed and got dusted every week. They had made feeble attempts to read it, but not finding the Old Testament very inspiring, they gave up trying to understand its purpose in their lives. Once Angie started her class, she sparked Dillon's interest and before long he started coming to the class and an unlikely life-long friendship was struck up between him and Jack Kough, a brilliant teacher with a PhD, while Dillon didn't even have a high school diploma.

Every weekend, Jack and his wife, Arlene, allowed the small church group to use their beautiful home for a Sunday service. About 50 people, including their pastor, Ken Wells, and his wife Billie, came to hear a sermon and fellowship. Angie and the kids still went to early Mass every Sunday. Then she and Dillon went together up to Jack's house for a non-denominational service.

It felt so right to worship together. On a particularly beautiful Sunday afternoon, Jack took Dillon over to an outside bench. He prayed the sinner's prayer with him and Dillon quietly accepted Jesus as his savior and lord.

For the next week, Dillon was very emotional. Talking about the crucifixion brought tears to his eyes. Angie wondered why the Lord had never given her such a profound experience. She was envious.

That evening, she decided to test the Lord. After Dillon went to sleep, she tip-toed back into the living room and knelt down beside the couch and repeated the sinner's prayer and waited and waited: nothing. Feeling foolish, she got up and then the thought occurred to her, *I've always believed and been faithful to the Lord, perhaps Dillon must have needed an extra crack on the head to get his attention.* Satisfied with her own explanation, she went back to bed.

Every Tuesday morning at six am, they met with some of the church people for an hour of prayer and meditation. They took short vacations to the ocean with Jack and Arlene, usually somewhere nearby like south to Pismo Beach or north to Fort Bragg.

Dillon discussed with Jack the benefits of adding a new experience to his life, and introduced him to the casinos. While walking thought the Poker tables, much to his embarrassment, Jack ran into a man whom he was counseling about a gambling addiction. After that, Jack decided that he could live without the new experience.

Jack, Arlene, and Angie

The blessed days were soon to end. Arlene woke one morning to find Jack sitting up in his favorite chair out on the porch. The coffee was still warm, Bible in his lap. He had died of a massive heart attack.

At the memorial service with the church people, Angie gave a tribute to their special friend Jack.

"How do we say what Jack meant to us? We loved him so. He is permanently etched in our lives. Our hearts ache when we think of popcorn or the funny stories he told or chicken at the Sugar Plum restaurant or of him sleeping in our recliner chair on Sunday afternoon watching football.

What pleasurable days we all spent together. How kind and gentle he was to our children. I'll always smile when I misuse the words picture and pitcher. Dillon boasted that Jack would never correct his grammar "'cause it's perfect."

Most of all we'll miss hearing the wonderful salvation messages on Tuesday night Bible Study. Jack brought the Bible alive for us, showed us how to cherish each word, how to devour its meaning and apply it to our lives, how to love it entirely.

I suppose God could have put someone else in our lives when we were seeking, but we're so grateful that Jack was obedient and self-giving of his time. He taught us and, slowly, but surely, line upon line, we learned. Several months before Jack died, he had each member of the class prepare a lesson and teach it.

We are no longer dependent on Jack to teach us. We know how to depend on the Holy Spirit to enlighten us. We know now how to seek answers or how to find comfort and joy from the Scriptures for ourselves. Isn't that the best reward for a teacher: that his students can carry on, reproducing his work?

So dear teacher, we recite for you, your best lesson:
We have a God who loves us very much.
Because of our sinfulness, we are separated from Him,
But God, in his loving kindness, provided us with a complete and perfect sacrifice,
His beloved son, Jesus Christ.
If we believe in Him and ask Him to be our Lord and Savior,
We are given the free gift of salvation.

Loretta Wilson

We are invited to join the family of God and we are promised eternal life.

I know that Jack would give us an A+. I also know that when our day comes to meet our Lord face to face, Jack will surely be there standing right there shouting, 'Hurry up! I could hardly wait for you to get here too.'

In thanksgiving for Jack, we make this commitment to the Lord: to speak out boldly over and over to whosoever will listen, telling them the Good News of Jesus Christ."

⊗⊗

Dillon had a long list of unusual friends. Jolly Jones worked with Dillon at Western Gravel and he was one of a kind. He was a mechanic who wrote poetry and also made beautiful knives and daggers. He dressed as a mountain man with his long hair past his shoulders. One of his knives was put on display at the LBJ Library in Austin Texas and two of his books of poetry were published.

Jimmy was fascinated by his Pop's friend, especially when Jolly pulled his belt buckle apart and it became an engraved knife, but he wasn't always happy with the company his Pop chose to keep. For instance, he was pretty upset when Dillon gave away his best sleeping bag to one of his homeless buddies who had stopped by the house to tell Dillon goodbye; he was leaving town and he was walking. When Jimmy complained, Dillon explained, "Remember son, but for the grace of God and your mother, go I."

 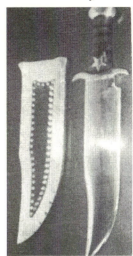

Jolly Jones and one of his knives

Another unique friend was Ed, a most compelling personality. Their friendship had begun in grade school. He lived 20 miles south in San Juan Bautista. Being a self-appointed sheriff, he wore a holster with a loaded pistol and patrolled the streets of San Juan.

He was unpredictable: sometimes showing up at their house on holidays, knowing there would be a good meal. Eda, Angie's mother, instantly disliked Ed when she caught him forking the best piece of meat to his plate while everyone had their eyes closed during the blessing.

Angie took her mother aside when she complained that he always showed up, uninvited at family gatherings. "Never you mind, Mama, this is Dillon's house and his friends are always welcome."

Eda just had to make one more comment about how the rolls had been counted out so there would be enough for everyone, after she noticed Ed had four on his plate. Angie shot her a look. "Mama, zip it, please."

Many years later, near the end of 2003, he called Dillon to ask him if he would buy his silver dollars that were buried in his backyard. "They're worth more, but I'll take dollar for dollar. I'm sure there will be enough to bury me. I've got cancer, so if you want to see me, you better come soon." Knowing Angie's business acumen, he asked her to handle the details.

They immediately drove over to San Juan Bautista to see and to help Ed dig up his yard. Roll after roll of silver dollars was uncovered, $2,700.00 worth, more than enough for his burial. They were wrapped in paper towel rolls with duct tape around each package. "You keep whatever is left over," he told them. "I want you to have all my recipes too. They're winners, every one."

Ed was a great dancer and loved music. He always carried two pencils in his pocket so that when music was playing, he could beat out the tempo on the edge of a table or a dashboard of a car. Dillon would surely miss him.

Ed's silver dollars, taped in paper towel rolls

Toward the end of his time, Ed was admitted to a hospice home in Monterey and Dillon and Angie took turns staying with him day and night. The nurse told them that sometimes he might hallucinate and not to be disturbed by what he said. Having heard the nurse's warning, Ed started mumbling about those "damn Indians over at the mission" who had stolen his blankets. He went on and listed all the items they had stolen. Angie and Dillon looked at each other, not knowing what to say until Ed started laughing and coughing. "If you like that one, I'll tell you another."

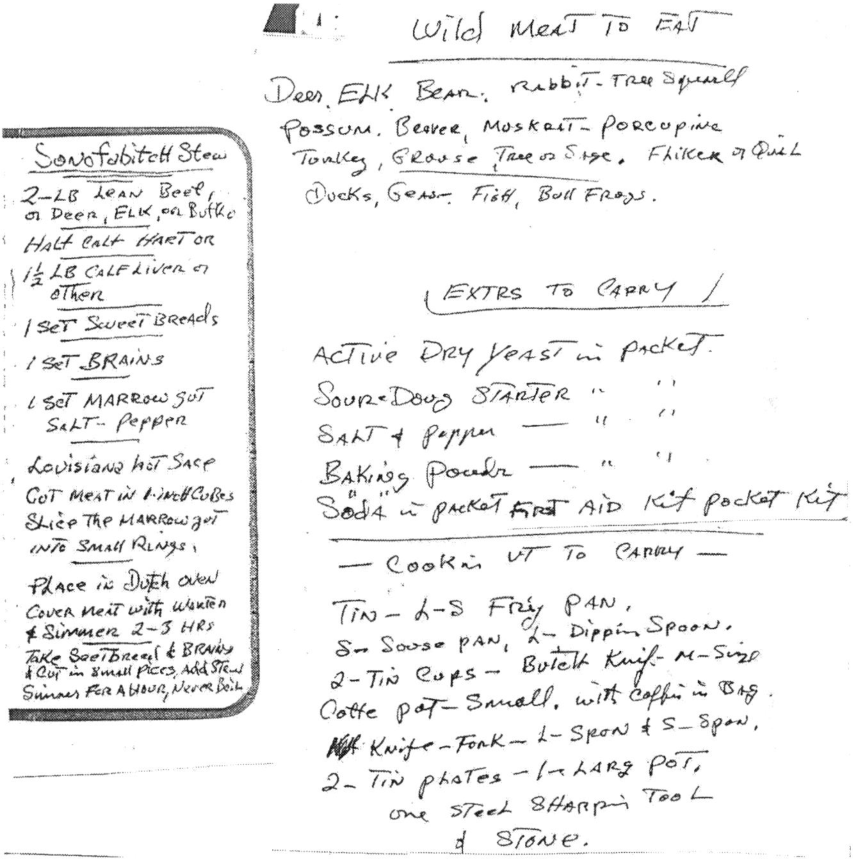
Sonofabitch Stew
2-LB Lean Beef, or Deer, Elk, or Buffalo
Half Calf Hart or
1½ LB Calf Liver or other
1 Set Sweet Breads
1 Set Brains
1 Set Marrow gut
Salt - Pepper
Louisiana hot Sace
Cut Meat in 1-inch Cubes
Slice the Marrow gut into Small Rings,
Place in Dutch oven
Cover Meat with Water & Simmer 2-3 HRS
Take Sweet Bread & Brains & Cut in small Pices, Add Stew
Simmer For A Hour, Never Boil

Wild Meat to Eat
Deer, Elk, Bear, Rabbit - Tree Squirrel
Possum, Beaver, Muskrat - Porcupine
Turkey, Grouse, Tree or Sage, Flicker or Quail
Ducks, Geese, Fish, Bull Frogs.

Extras to Carry
Active Dry Yeast in packet.
Sour Dough Starter " "
Salt & Pepper — " "
Baking Powder — " "
Soda in packet First Aid Kit pocket Kit

— Cookin ut to Carry —
Tin - L-S Fry Pan,
S- Souse Pan, L- Dippin Spoon,
2-Tin Cups - Butch Knife M-Size
Coffe pot - Small, with Coffie in Bag.
Knife - Fork - L- Spoon & S- Spoon,
2- Tin plates - 1- Larg pot,
one Steel Sharpin Tool
& Stone.

One of Ed's recipes

ঔ

Late one night, Angie answered the phone to hear Eda say, "Rico was taken to the hospital. It's his time."

"What are you saying, Mama?"

"Angela, he's old. He's smoked too many cigarettes. He can't breathe anymore. It's his time. I'm at the hospital, but I'm going home now to find some paper."

It shocked Angie that her mother could talk so casually about her father dying. *Was she already looking for the insurance papers?*

By the time Angie got to the hospital, Rico was semi-conscious and had been placed in an oxygen tent. All she wanted to do was to reach in and hug him. Serafina and Laetitia were already there. Dillon had stayed home with the children, saying he would come when she needed him.

It was an hour before Eda returned. She was slapping some papers in her hand, waving them at her daughters, she cried, "Love letters, from the putana." During World War II Rico was gone for four whole years. He was Port Commander in Juneau, Alaska. "You know, every now and then a woman called the house and asked for the Colonel. Ha! Now I know who called. It was the putana! Love letters from the putana. He saved them!"

Laetitia asked quietly, "What's a putana?"

Eda heard her and answered none too quietly, "A whore! The putana is a whore. He betrayed me!"

Angie had never seen her mother so enraged or dramatic. She ripped open the oxygen tent and waved the papers in front of Rico's face. "Open your eyes, Rico. Look what I'm holding. Why did you save these? Did you love the putana?" She was shouting. Angie got up to close the door; else the whole hospital would hear her.

Rico, eyes still closed, breathing with difficulty, barely got out the words, "Will you forgive me?"

"No," shouted Eda.

That night, Rico passed away, probably to avoid another confrontation with Eda.

Planning a funeral was a new experience for the three sisters. Eda wanted no part of it. "You girls bury him if you want. I don't care if he rots." She did give him a suit to wear. "There are only a few stains on it. No one will notice." Angie spotted the stains.

Still single, Serafina flirted shamelessly with the funeral director. Laetitia was in charge of calling the family and friends and notifying the Knights of Columbus, Elks Lodge, and other organizations that Rico had belonged to. The burial affair was coming together.

The night of the rosary, the family came in early. Rico looked handsome, even in death. One by one, the girls kissed their beloved father goodbye. When Eda came in, she leaned over the coffin. The girls were relieved to see she was over her anger and was about to kiss him. But, no, she brought out a razor, and with a quick slash, shaved off half of his moustache.

"Mama! How could you do that?"

"Don't worry. No one will notice." She was smiling.

Dillon turned and whispered to Angie. "Angel, you can't let your father be humiliated. He doesn't deserve that."

"What can I do?" she whispered back. "Please go fix him."

Dillon raced to the nearest drugstore, bought a razor, and finished off the rest of the moustache, just as the Knights of Columbus were marching in dressed in full regalia, including their swords.

Angela, Serafina, and Laetitia covered their faces with their hands. Their shoulders were shaking. The whispers could be heard, "Look how they grieve for their papa. Do you see their tears? How beautiful." Actually, they were trying hard not to laugh out loud after Eda said it was so nice to see young men joining the Knights. Clearly, all the Knights were over 70 years old, stumbling down the aisle, nearly stabbing each other with their swords.

Then came the Elks with the chiming bells, calling out Rico's name, only to proclaim, "He does not answer." These memorial rituals were so meaningful to the old time members, but the younger generation didn't appreciate the significance.

Dillon leaned over to Angie, "I'll haunt you forever if you give me a funeral like this."

Back at the house, Eda asked everyone to gather around the piano. On the wall hung a huge oil painting of Rico, smoking his pipe. She raised a glass of wine and toasted him, "Rest in peace, Rico." The sisters fully expected her to down the wine and dramatically toss the glass into the fireplace, but she didn't. Her anger was gone and she simply said, "Mangia. Let's eat." Then the food came out, lots of food. In memory of Rico, the family and friends ate drank and were merry 'til late in the night.

The week after the funeral, Eda continued to have 3:00 Sunday lunch. Grandma and Grandpa Savio had died. Grandma Divencenzi had lived to be 96. She died from an ulcer, only because the hospital thought she was too old to treat. Even with the older generation gone, it was mandatory that the family gathering continue.

Chapter 14

1980-1998

Dillon was drinking heavily every day. Some days he would sit and brood for hours. When she tried to talk to him, he got up and walked away. Come night time, even with his drinking, he was still able to make love to Angela. He appeased her by always telling her how much he loved her and always thanked her for being his wife. Angie didn't know how to help him get off the pain pills and beer.

The pharmacist tried to tell Dillon that he was taking too many Ativan, Vicodin, and Tylenol with codeine, and would surely become addicted to them. "What's the matter with your doctor?" he questioned him.

Dillon told the pharmacist to stick it where the sun don't shine and to mind his own business. He suspected that his doctor was an addict himself. He would prescribe bottles of 100 pills whenever the prescription needed to be refilled.

Dillon was taking six to eight Vicodin each day, along with six to ten cans of beer, an entire case on the weekend.

Angie thought back to what the counselor had told her, "No more threats—just leave him."

When she announced she was leaving, he begged her to stay, getting teary-eyed. "Angel, you know I can't live without you. I'll quit." Sounding desperate, he cried, "Look, I won't take anymore pills." He flushed every last pill down the toilet, blood pressure pills included.

Angie covered her ears. "I can't live like this any longer." She rushed out before he could change her mind. She cried all the way to Serafina's. All these years she never went home to Eda and Rico. She knew they would sympathize with her and tell her to throw the bum out and come home. She didn't want them to think badly of Dillon, so she always went to Serafina's house. There she could cry and complain all she needed, and Sera would still love Dillon.

She called her oldest daughter Julie and asked her to go check on her father. "I have to know he's okay."

Julie was a nurse and could see how very sick Dillon was when she got to her parent's house. His eyes were red and puffy and he was hunched over in a chair.

"She left me Julie. She really left me. How can I go on without her?" His hands were shaking.

"Pop, you're very sick. You need to stop drinking or you're going to die. You're not nice to be around when you drink; that's why Mom left." Julie knew that she had to be really honest with him. "If you want her back, you have to go get help with your drinking problem and not take any more pills."

Dillon got through the night, shaking and vomiting. Making his way to the kitchen the next morning, he put on a pot of coffee and glanced at the paper on the counter. The first sentence read, "Let us help you get over your addiction." Dillon read the whole article. In later years Angela would credit that moment to "the hand of God." No one ever admitted to putting the paper there.

Dillon reluctantly called the phone number right away and asked, "If I come there, do you promise me I'll be out of pain?"

The man that answered said, "We promise you nothing. That's not how it works." A little kinder, he added, "Come on over and let's talk."

Dillon got dressed. He was afraid to go and more afraid not to go. The building was only a few miles away. He parked in front and sat in his car for a long while, wanting a beer so badly. He had his Bible on his lap. The sign over the door of the building read, "Monte Villa". Dillon made up his mind, and walked through the front door, bringing his Bible with him.

"Biblical Description of Alcoholism"
Proverbs 23:29-35 New American Standard

Who has woe? Who has sorrow?
Who has contentions? Who has complaining?
Who has wounds without cause?
Who has redness of eyes?
Those who linger long over wine,
Those who go to taste mixed wine.
Do not look on the wine when it is red,
When it sparkles in the cup,
When it goes down smoothly;
At the last it bites like a serpent
And stings like a viper.
Your eyes will see strange things
And your mind will utter perverse things.
And you will be like one who lies down in the middle of the sea,
Or like one who lies down on the top of the mast.
They stuck me, but I did not become ill;
They beat me, but I did not know it.
When shall I awake?
I shall seek another drink.

All the personnel who worked at Monte Villa were AA members. The counselor greeted Dillon, "Welcome. What can I do for you?"

"I'm here to get un-addicted."

The man smiled, "Well, we're glad you're here. Come on in to my office and we'll talk." He could see that Dillon's hands were shaking.

Together they filled out the forms. "I see you have insurance," the man pointed out. "That's good. We have a physician on staff. He'll want to give you a complete physical. There's one thing I'll have to ask of you."

"What's that?"

"That you leave your Bible in the car. We replace it with what we call "The Big Book." For the next 30 days, we become your family and we supply you with reading material.

Remember, there are no locked doors here. You voluntarily walked in here and at any point during your stay, you can walk out. But remember this too: we're here for you. We've all been through this and we walk every step with you to get you, as you put it, 'un-addicted.'" He smiled at that word. "I'm going to contact your family and tell them you are here and assure them you're well cared for. They need to know too, that letters and occasional phone calls are fine, but we discourage visits. We want to remove you from your usual environment and only concentrate on getting you 'un-addicted.'" The man smiled again, decided that he would have to adopt that word for future use.

There was a knock at the door. "Come in, Doc," the counselor called out. "Dillon McCandless, shake hands with Dr. Callahan, he's our resident physician." The man standing in the doorway was short and stocky with twinkling, mischievous eyes and a ruddy complexion.

"Are you an alcoholic too?" asked Dillon, speaking up for the first time in a while.

The doctor laughed. "Are you kidding? Didn't you catch my name? You must know how we Irish like to drink." He emphasized an Irish brogue.

"I'm Scottish."

The doctor laughed again. "Same difference. Oh how I remember the green Guinness on St. Paddy's Day. Got myself thrown in the slammer, almost lost my license."

While Dr. Callahan talked, he observed Dillon's appearance, taking note of his shaking hands, his bloodshot eyes, and sallow complexion.

"We'll have lots of time to reminisce. Now let's get to that physical exam." He led Dillon to an exam room the walls covered with several inspirational posters and an exam table against one wall. Dillon undressed, put on a gown, and lay down on the table.

Dr. Callahan gently traced his hand over all the scars on Dillon's legs. He commented sadly, "You paid a big price for the drinks that caused this."

Dillon just nodded. *This man really understands,* he thought. *I just might stay here thirty days, but how will I make it without seeing my Angel.* The troublesome thoughts rolled around his head. He wondered if she was thinking about him. *Does she even miss me?* He surely missed her.

The doctor gave him a mild sedative to relax him and prescribed some blood pressure medication.

Dillon was then led to his room and introduced to his roommate for the next few weeks, Felix Chavez. He was short, but well built. He walked with a swagger, hitching his Levi's up every few steps. Dillon would observe him meticulously trimming his moustache every morning. He told Dillon, "You worry too much about your woman. A good looking guy like you, I know she'll be waiting for you."

At one of the group sessions, Felix claimed he drank because his wife cheated on him. When asked if he ever cheated on her, he snorted, "Of course! I'm the man. They expect us to cheat on them." From then on, the rehab group dubbed him Felix, "the Macho Mexican."

Also in residence was the bank manager. His employees cared enough about him to stage an intervention, He was shocked when they told him of his behavior at the bank when he had been drinking. He had thought no one noticed. The group called him "Classy Dude," because every day he dressed in a suit and tie like he was going to the bank.

No one expected Jane, an older woman, to make it through the program. She couldn't sit still during the group sessions and would wander around the room, softly humming to herself, not participating. She had been on Ativan and vodka for years. They affectionately called her "the Dancing Doll." She left two weeks into her session. It was a sobering day when the group was told she had overdosed.

Tim was there for a second session. His insurance company was paying Monte Villa to keep "Two-times Tim" another 30 days. "I just like the three square meals a day," he winked. "It's a paid vacation."

Dillon was christened "Serious Scott," because he was always studying "The Big Book," doing each assignment like his life depended on it.

There were 30 men and women in residence. It was soon evident that most blamed someone else for their drinking or drug problems. They were admonished to not start any romantic relationships with each other, as it would be harmful to their recovery. Even so, there were those who engaged in a quickie some nights, sneaking into each other's rooms.

After a few days, the 12 Steps were introduced. There were guest speakers, lectures, and group sessions, where they bared their souls and told of their worst deeds. Dillon thought he was a saint compared to some of the other residents. He soon learned that the women liked to embellish their stories, while the men seemed to minimize their actions.

Physical exercise was introduced as part of their very busy schedule. It was intended that they be exhausted by the end of the day and would have no trouble sleeping.

Dillon's struggled most with the final few steps that involved makings amends to those you have hurt. He was assigned the task of writing a letter to each of his immediate family members, telling them what they meant to him and admitting the sorrow his drinking had caused them, ending with an actual love letter to each of them.

He agonized over every word, knowing that he would have to read these letters out loud to each of his children and, especially, his wife, in front of everyone.

Dillon cherished the few letters Angie wrote to him. He didn't want to tell her what he was doing and she didn't ask. When he talked to her on the phone it was a strained conversation. She then broke the unwelcomed news to him that she was going to take a vacation with her Ya-Ya friends. They had signed up for a 17 day Perillo tour along the western coast of Italy.

Dillon panicked inside, so afraid he was losing her. All he said was, "I want you to have a good time. I'll be here when you come home. Then we'll talk. Be careful. I love you."
He got little sleep that night.

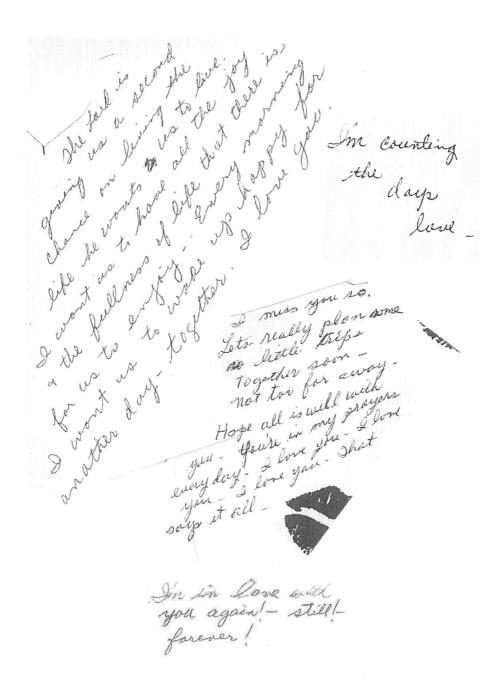

I love you – I love you
I love you!!! xxxooo.
I made the arrangement myself.
Last night I was reading
my papers from Monte Vill,
& it said – "No Conjugal visits" –
Do you suppose you could
unlock the window?
I am feeling so strong
about all thats happened.
Sometimes I feel such wonderful
relief – like a big nightmare
is over – then I get real scared
that nothing will really
change and well go back to
the way things have been far so

long – I want to believe
this is a real beginning for
us – I know we can have
a wonderful life together
because you know what a
special love we have always
had for each other – nothing can
change that. My heart actually
starts to pound when I think
of you. It <u>actually</u> does still do
that after all these years –
I will see you tonight
after the classes – 9:30 I think –
Ed Leal come over – He was
really concerned – wanted to come see
you right away – I told him maybe
later – you know – he's a good friend
to you –
Love.

8/28/87

This is my last letter to you in treatment.

I can't tell you how proud I am of you.

What you have achieved it is a miracle!

I know now that you are capable of doing what ever you set your mind to.

You absolutely amazed me — See you Tues. 12:00 —

Get ready for our new, loving, exciting life to gether.

I love you,

Chapter 15

Checking into their first hotel in Palermo, Angie and her friends were breathless with excitement and were having a difficult time believing they were really in Italy. Their rooms were not too impressive. They were actually rather shabby; however, they soon came to realize that each night the accommodations would improve, right up to the last night of the tour, when they would spend the night at the stunning Pope's Palace in Rome, everything trimmed in gold.

Angie's friend Marie had organized the trip. They always put her in charge of making all the arrangements. She had her own bookkeeping business and she, like Angie, knew how to stretch a dollar.

Nancy was partially deaf, but was proficient at lip reading. The other girls tried to remember to always be facing her when they spoke and to keep their hands away from their mouths. She had an executive position at PacBell and always worried that she would be fired as her hearing started to fail. "Are you kidding?" her friends would tell her. "Big companies love their top employees with disabilities. It improves their public image." When she fessed up and told her employer that she had difficulty hearing, they gave her an assistant who traveled with her.

Dorothy, whom the other girls called Toby, was tiny. Angela felt like a giant standing next to her. She was an executive of business services. She was sweet tempered and agreeable to all the traveling decisions.

Loretta Wilson

Poor Jeannie was the only liberal Democrat among her conservative Republican friends. They agreed to never talk politics, especially while on vacation, lest their life-long friendship be damaged. Jeannie was Angie's oldest friend. They started Kindergarten together and often stayed overnight at each other's home. In the second grade, down in the Divencenzi's basement, they became blood sisters, pricking their index fingers and joining the blood. Now in their late 30s, they were touring Italy together.

Sitting on the bed of their first hotel room, Toby was reading the itinerary for the next day, when Angie walked back in from the hallway. She was very quiet, looking out the window. The Ya-Yas exchanged looks.

Angie announced that she was going to shower and go to bed, and that she would be careful not to use up all the hot water. When she left the room, the buzzing began. Something was definitely wrong. The girls all wondered why she wouldn't tell them. Usually, the girls had no problem sharing their troubles with each other. She had hardly talked on the plane ride and now she was going to bed early. Something must be very wrong. The girls decided her silence would have to end, even if they had to force words out of her. This trip was their fun vacation not a funeral.

"Maybe they're getting a divorce," Nancy whispered sadly, not wanting Angie to hear her over the sound of the running shower.

The other two wouldn't believe it. "Naw. Impossible. Not those two. Gag me with a spoon. They're probably still making out in the back seat of a car on Friday nights."

The discussion continued until Angie came out to say goodnight in her slippers and bathrobe. They noticed her puffy eyes.

In unison they shouted at her, "Sit down." Stunned by their tone, Angie sat down on the edge of the room's couch.

"Are we your best friends?" said Marie taking the lead on the conversation.

"Of course. You know you are," said Angie, taken aback by their ambush.

"Do you trust us?"

"Of course. That's a silly question."

"Then tell us what's going on."

Angie burst into tears. Through the blubbering, crying and hiccupping, she spent two hours pouring out her heart, every detail from the last 18 years.

"The cad."

"The brute! How could you stay with him?"

Angela jumped up from the couch. "See! That's why I didn't tell you! I didn't want you to think badly of Dillon. You know how much I love him. I always will. What I've been reading about is the co-dependent." She pointed to herself. "That's me. It says that I'm as sick as an alcoholic and sometimes responsible for the person drinking more."

"My God. Now she's going to blame herself for his drunkenness. Angie, listen up." Marie spoke for all of them. "It's good he's in rehab. Let the professionals help him get through this. You are not responsible and you can't cure him, so we are going to make you have fun on this vacation, whether you want it or not. Got that?"

"And guess what!" said Toby, "We'll still love Dillon too, 'cause he's yours."

Only Jeannie said nothing, having dealt with the shame of alcoholism in her family. She didn't have anything bad to say about Dillon. With her Irish last name of Murphy, she always thought it was appropriate to send Dillon, the Scotsman, a St. Patrick's Day card every year. He liked to argue with her as to who was smarter, better looking, and more courageous: the Irish or the Scotts.

Before they retired for the night, all five of the women hugged and in a tight circle, they cried and prayed together.

"Friends forever," said Nancy.

Loretta Wilson

The next morning, they began a series of tours by boarding a large bus that would take them around Sicily, to southern Italy, along the western coast, and two weeks later, ending with a multi-day tour of Rome. Each day the bus drove them to see beautiful destinations, crowded tourist areas and show them the best places to eat.

One of their first tours took the Ya-Yas from Palermo down to the Strait of Messina. The Sicilians were such handsome people, from the very dark skin and curly hair to the very fair blue-eyed blondes.

Their tour director, Marcello, talked constantly his hands flying to emphasize the history lesson. "The reason the people of Sicily are so varied is because all other countries sailed through the Strait of Messina, up along Italy to invade Europe and they stopped in Sicily along the way." Marcello gave them a half smile, let out a low whistle, and let them know what they were doing along the way.

Almost every day, Marie and Angie shared a beer and pizza with thick bread and spicy sauce. Sometimes they ordered pasta puttanesca, which meant Harlot's Pasta, as they learned from Marcello.

The tour arranged dinners at local restaurants every night. Most were seven courses of extraordinary cuisine. Entertainment for the evening was violin or an accordion player, and sometimes an opera singer. The Italians considered the evening meal the best part of the day. It sometimes took up to two hours of eating, drinking, and talking before the meal was finished. Never rushing, it was always a time to relax.

Among their tour group were several Mafioso-type men, all with young beautiful women who, everyone could tell, were not their wives. The men all wore a gold goat's horn on a chain and lavished the women with expensive souvenirs and jewelry. When the group ate at restaurants, the men were so rude to the waiters, often shouting at them to bring more vino. They were the perfect examples of the "ugly Americans."

After traveling to mainland Italy and moving north, the bus drove along the western side of Italy, up the Amalfi Coast. It was a harrowing experience, driving along a sheer drop-off on a narrow road. It was especially terrifying when they met another bus coming from the other direction. Toby shut her eyes and couldn't catch her breath. They had to remind her to keep breathing.

When visiting Pompeii, the tour group stopped at a museum near Mt. Vesuvius to see the petrified bodies on display in glass cases: the remains of ancient citizens preserved from the fatal eruption.

Then, on they traveled to Naples to see a musical show. During one of the songs, a handsome young man came down the aisle to their table and held out his hand to Angie. "Signora?" She got out of her seat and went with him up to the stage to dance the tarantella with the group of performers. Angie was sure her friends had arranged this.

Their final accommodation was across the street from the U.S. Embassy in Rome. Marcello arranged for them to visit the Capuchin cemetery located in the crypt beneath the Church of the Immaculate Conception. The whole room, including the chandeliers, was decorated with the bones of the monks who once resided there. The tour made them all shiver.

Angie bought herself a large pendant of Murano glass and other gifts for Serafina and Laetitia.

Angie and the Ya-Yas each took turns taking pictures with the Carabinieri: the well-dressed policemen of Italy.

When sightseeing, Angie stood on the viewing balcony and looked down into the Colosseum. She could imagine the gladiators and hear the clashing of their swords. There was just so much history to see, regardless of where they traveled in Italy.

Each day in Rome was a treasure of sights.

Wanting to be alone for a while, Angie walked down the street. While she admired the old buildings, a young girl ran up to her. "Oh look!" she pointed to a gold ring lying on the ground. The girl picked it up and tried it on. In broken English, she said, "No fit. For you signora." Grabbing Angie's hand, she put it on her finger. Angie didn't know what to say, so she just said "Thank you." As the young Italian girl was walking away, she looked back and called out, asking Angie for some money, again in broken English. Once again, Angie didn't know what to say so she just paid the little girl.

Turning the corner at the next block, another girl ran up to her, "Oh, look," and pointed to another gold ring lying on the ground: the scam of the day. By the end of the day, the gold ring had turned Angie's finger green.

Angie's favorite place on the tour was the Sistine Chapel. She stared in awe at Michelangelo's huge painting of God and the people going up to Heaven or down to the devil in Hell. Marcello told the story that when Michelangelo left town, the cardinal had clothes painted on the naked people. Upon his return, the emotional artist was so inflamed that his masterpiece had been vandalized that he repainted the devil to have the face of the cardinal.

Angie could have stayed there all day, but there were four saints being canonized in Rome that day and the crowds were huge. People were being ushered through the chapel in long lines, so there wasn't a chance to stay too long.

After three weeks of adventures, it was time to go home. Home to Dillon.

Other Alumnae News

The Ya-Ya Girls, all members of the class of 1956, recently spent 18 days touring Italy. Here they are in front of the ruins at the Coliseum in Rome. Next year, England, Ireland and Scotland!

The Ya-Ya Friends

(left) Jeannie, Angie, Nancy, Toby, and Marie, traveling to Italy

(right) The Ya-Yas, over 75 years old, and still traveling. (back) Marie, Angie, Nancy, (bottom) Toby, Jeannie

(left) Caroline, Angie, Marie, Joan, and Toby

Chapter 16

During the last week of rehab, the family was invited to come in for group sessions without Dillon. They sat for hours all together being counseled on how their lives would be different. Anxiety built up in Angie, as she thought about how she would soon see Dillon. At one session, she forgot how to exhale. The counselor could see she was about to faint. Taking Angie aside, she talked her through a breathing exercise. Breathe in, breathe out.

Each family member was instructed to write their feelings about Dillon. "Tell the worst of how his drinking affected you." Their letters would be read to him in front of all the residents. Angie thought she couldn't possibly embarrass Dillon like that, but once she got started writing, she polished off six pages. One painful memory just led her to another.

The day of Dillon's graduation from the program finally came. Having not seen each other for a month, it was as if he and Angie were meeting for the first time, all over again. All they could do was stare at each other. They ran into each other's arms, crying, kissing, hugging, touching, touching, always touching.

In a gravelly tone, he whispered, "Just wait until I get you home."

Counselors and residents gathered in a huge circle. Two chairs were placed in the middle. Dillon sat in one and, one by one, each family member sat in the other. Facing each other, knees almost touching, they read their letters. Dillon was instructed to not reply or argue with whatever they said, just listen.

Julie wanted to go first, to get it over with. She cited a few hurtful times, but her letter was short and she ended with, "I love you Daddy."

Jill's main complaint was that she thought Dillon was sometimes unfair and mean to her brother. She was the least affected by his drinking. Whenever he was mouthing off or shouting, she got on her horse and left to go riding for the day, returning when the household had settled down.

Jimmy refused to write a letter saying it was a waste of time. "Pop's just gonna drink again;" however, once he sat in the chair, he really let him have it, sometimes shouting at Dillon. "Why do you think I excelled in basketball? I wanted you to come to the games to see me play. You never came." Even though Julie, Jill, and Jimmy were adults, this session brought back painful memories they had from growing up.

Angie went last. She wrote about the hurtful times when he would blow up over minor things and ruin plans they had made and drive home erratically. On and on she went, reminding him of each event in detail.

Tears rolled down Dillon's cheek. He wanted to grab her hand and tell her how sorry he was. That was not allowed. No touching while she read.

When she had finished, there was a fire in a barrel out on the patio waiting for them. They all walked outside together with their letters to burn them. Dillon then read to each of them the love letters that he had written.

To Julie, he told her how beautiful she was with those, yellow-brown eyes like her mother.

To Jill, he told her how she was always smiling and happy with her animals.

To Jimmy, he began with, "My son, my son, my only son. No one could have a better son."

The longest letter was to Angie, telling her she was his inner strength, his very soul. He thanked her again for being his wife, ending with, "I'll love you forever with all my heart."

One of the counselors told Angie that he had stayed up all night writing his letters. They had to be just right.

Driving home that afternoon after the ceremony, the car was so quiet. No one knew what to expect. Finally, Julie spoke up, "Pop, we planned to take you to a real fancy restaurant to celebrate your homecoming." Angie could see he was unhappy with that announcement. She whispered harshly, "Don't you dare disappoint them. It was planned long ago."

Dillon got through the afternoon and, once home and back in their bedroom, he lay down next to Angela and said, "Later on, we'll get with it, but right now, just hold me. I've missed you so. I need to feel you. Just hold me. Let me touch you." Touching, touching always touching.

The family settled into a normal routine, minus the drinking. A good deal of Dillon's time revolved around daily AA meetings. Angie, of course, did not attend the meetings, but she did help plan the barbeques for members and their families.

Dillon regularly had his fellow AA members over to the house. Some became lifelong friends, especially Toothpick Jim, who always had a toothpick in his mouth. The two of them had recovery in common. Toothpick Jim acted as sponsor to some members. His advice was simple. "If you want to stay sober, just don't drink." When someone was tempted to drink, they knew to come to Dillon's house. Angie would make a big pot of coffee and leave the room. Dillon, Toothpick Jim, and the others talked, laughed, told war stories half of the night away. Dillon loved these unlovable guys. He was tough, yet so tender. His new license plate read, "Happy—Joyous and Free."

On one afternoon, Dillon was chairing a meeting. As Dillon led the meeting inside, Angie was outside setting the table for the barbeque. Through an open window she heard Dillon say, "I raised her from a pup." She inhaled sharply. *That's me he's talking about!* She resented his remark and made sure he knew it. "I was not your pup!" she yelled from outside the window.

She heard him laugh from inside the house. He was amused to hear her respond in an angry tone: a new side of her he had never seen before. "Oh Angel, I was just illustrating how young we were."

While driving into town one day, a young man in the car beside them kept honking his horn, shouting vulgar suggestions, flirting with Angie, being obnoxious. Without thinking, Angie flipped him the bird.

Dillon stared at her. "Hot damn Angel, I've waited a lifetime to see you show some pizazz."

Red cheeked with embarrassment, she had to admit, it felt pretty good.

They had to adjust to each other as two new and different people. Dillon still had a temper, but had learned to control it. Most of the time.

After one of their disagreements, he ripped up the love letter he had written. Immediately, he knew he had gone too far. That letter was so special to Angie. She had kept it in a little box on the dresser. Grabbing the scotch tape, he painstakingly pieced it all together. The next time she looked in the box, there was a note on top. "I will always mean every word in the letter. Please forgive my temper. I'll try harder. I love you."

CʒᏰꙨ

Loretta Wilson

All too soon, the children grew up, married, and were out on their own. Julie married Ken, a contractor. Jill married Steve, a union carpenter—Dillon walked her down the aisle on crutches, having just had another knee replacement. Jimmy was 34 years old when he finally found the perfect wife, Christie. He had a good job with an environmental heating and sheet metal company. All the children found great spouses.

A couple of days after Jim and Christie's wedding, the whole family flew down to Cabo San Lucas, Mexico. The newlyweds usually went off on their own during the day, but most nights, the whole family ate together. The young couples rented jet skis to ride the waves in the Sea of Cortez. They ate quesadillas, tacos, and enchiladas, all the usual Mexican foods.

Dillon rarely deviated from what he wore. His usual was a snap button shirts, Levi's, and boots. Occasionally, he wore a bathing suit, but just to swim in. He got dressed immediately after he was finished in the water. None of the family could believe it when he came down for dinner one night, looking like a professional tourist, wearing a tank top, bright green shorts, blue socks with his flip flops, and a sombrero on his head. Angie warned the kids, "Don't any of you laugh." The vacation was full of memories they would never forget.

Back home, Dillon and Angie were satisfied to know all the children were happily married. Taking some credit, thinking, *Maybe we didn't do so badly after all.*

130

(above) Julie and Jill
(below) Jill and Dillon

(above) Julie and Ken
(below) Dillon and Jill

(left) Jill and Steve
(below) Dillon and Jimmy

(left) Jim and Christie
(below) the whole
family on vacation in
Cabo

In total, the McCandless children presented them with seven grandchildren, and so, on Sunday afternoons, the house was still full of family. Angie now cooked for the traditional family gathering, since Eda was getting up in years. Life continued to roll on.

Jacob McCandless died peacefully and he was buried quietly with no fanfare. Just the way he wanted it. He was buried next to his wife at Mt. Hope Cemetery with only the immediate family present.

In February of 1989, Eda was in the hospital with some non-life threatening problems. Three days, before Valentine's Day, she called Angela, "I'm going to die this week."

"Mama, you can't die this week, I'm too busy at the flower shop." She didn't believe Eda was serious.

"Well, I don't want to leave you girls, but it's my time, so I'll die this week."

Serafina, Laetitia, and Angela, dutifully went to be with her. Out in the hall, the doctor approached the girls. "You know, I didn't think your mother was that critical, but she is old, 92, I believe, and if she makes up her mind to die, she just might. Dr. Silva was smiling when he told them, pointing to his face, "I just grew this moustache and she told me I looked like Hitler. She's my favorite patient."

That week, Serafina had called in her friend Beatrice to see Eda's aura. She was a little woman with a bun on top of her head. It looked like an ice bag to Angie. Sera was into meditation and new age religion. Beatrice would interpret the auras she saw around people. She claimed this helped to know oneself. She perused all the people in the room. When she came to Angie, she sucked in her breath. "A most unusual aura. Your colors go from the most debased red to the highest spiritual color of lavender, a most unusual aura." Angie was satisfied with that interpretation. *Dillon would love the red color best,* she thought.

After that, Beatrice sat in the corner, putting her finger tips together. With her eyes closed, she began to rock back and forth and softly hummed, "Ohmmmmm."

Laetitia and Dale, the seminary man, sat in another corner of the room, holding hands. They no longer attended the Catholic Church, but had switched to the Episcopal faith. Their pastor was there along with Eda's Catholic pastor.

Clearly, Eda was enjoying all the attention. Suddenly, she sat up, raised her arms, stared at the ceiling, and spoke out loud, "There's Papa—oh, there's Mama." Then, looking back and forth, she asked, "Where's Rico?"

The girls exchanged looks; they knew how dramatic their mother could be, but was she really seeing the here-after?

"Daddy's probably hiding from her," Laetitia whispered, with a small laugh.

Eda lay back down. Her last words, before she closed her eyes, were "Don't forget the ham." Her breathing became labored and she seemed agitated. Dr. Silva said her heart was beating erratically. He prescribed some morphine be given to her. It settled her down and within an hour, she had passed away.

They gave her as an elaborate funeral as they could; she'd like that. They dressed her in the elegant dress she had bought for her 90th birthday party, as she had requested. She had paid an enormous price for it, but told the girls they could get the money's worth out of it by putting it on her in her casket. She had also requested a nice casket, but not too nice, "Don't let Serafina pick it out, she'll spend too much, and don't forget the funeral home always gives a ham to the family."

Sera was again flirting with the funeral director, when Angie, anticipating what she was about to say, slapped her hand over Sera's mouth. "Don't say one word about the damn ham."

The girls arranged for the traditional rosary to be held the night before burial. The next morning, the casket was brought to the church for a High Mass, with the incense floating up to Heaven and a full choir singing her favorite hymns, particularly, Ave Maria. She was buried next to Rico at the Santa Clara Catholic Cemetery. All the Italian relatives were buried there. Shortly before she died, Eda took Angela to the cemetery for a tour, telling her little stories about each relative. The trunk of the car was filled with coffee cans stuffed with ice plant to hold the flowers up. She put cactus flowers on her mother-in-laws grave and did not say a prayer for her, but instead pointing to the headstone with her cane, saying only, "I forgive you."

Special flowers were placed on Grandma and Grandpa Savio's grave, along with prayers for them. Angie was walking around reading the tombstones, when she glanced over to see Eda kneeling down on top of Rico's grave. Touched by the sight, Angie thought, *She's going to kiss Papa's grave*, but then Eda hollered out, "Get over here. I can't get up." Disappointed, Angie realized she had only been cutting the grass around the stone. There was still no forgiveness for Rico, no kiss, no flowers, no prayer.

Now that she had passed away too, Eda would lie there with Rico, for the rest of time. She had commissioned Angie to keep up the tradition of putting flowers on the graves "at least on Memorial Day. Don't embarrass the family."

Chapter 17

Their 30th anniversary was coming up. Dillon asked Angie if she wanted something special.

"What I really want is for you to come to Mass with me, just one time. That would be very special to me."

Other than being married in the Catholic church, a few funerals, and of course, the children's First Holy Communion, Dillon had not stepped foot in the church in years.

He agreed to go, but only if they went to Mass during the week, when only a few people attended.

Father Dan spotted them sitting in the last pew at the back of the church. He approached them and asked what the occasion was.

When told it was their 30th anniversary, he ushered them up to the altar where he invited them to repeat their marriage vows. He began his talk, telling Dillon that he knew how difficult it must be living with Angie. He commended him for his grace and fortitude to stay married to her for 30 years.

Dillon appreciated that pastor's sense of humor and from then on, had nothing but good things to say about Fr. Dan, a special priest and a special friend.

Going to Mass with Dillon was indeed a treasured gift to Angie; she only wished she had remembered to invite the children to witness this rare occasion.

ᬧᬗ

Now that the kids were grown, Dillon and Angie were all alone in the house. Wanting to enjoy Dillon's sobriety, they decided to buy a motorhome and drive off for as long as they wanted. They could afford it. Dillon had done well picking real estate properties to buy and sell, and with the sale of the shop giving them income from rent.

They bought a motorhome, and they were ready to go. The first big trip was to Mexico. They drove all the way down to Cabo San Lucas, over 1,000 miles. They traveled with Dillon's old friends, Jim and Leone Alter, and then picked up three other couples who didn't want to travel alone.

One couple was Bill and Sybil Clemmons. They hailed from North Carolina, bringing with them their strong Southern accents, finger licking corn bread, and a relaxed attitude.

Next came Jim and Cathy Livesley, from Southern California. Jim was a retired air force lieutenant colonel. He was tough, having been involved in the rescue attempt of our prisoners in Iran during the Carter administration. Dillon especially enjoyed his company and appreciated his unusual sense of humor, which was so like his own.

The last couple to sign on was Virginia and Elmer Stepanek, both school teachers from the San Diego area. They brought school supplies with them to distribute to the Mexican children. Elmer was on a mission to teach the children why they should not throw their trash on the ground. He failed.

The caravan stayed down in Mexico for over a month. Dillon had always called Angie his hummingbird, because she was always flitting around, cleaning the house or whatever, but after their trip to Mexico, and learning how to say it in Spanish, he switched to calling her "la chupa rosa."

Their Spanish was sufficient, but not great. The group was careful not to drink the water, but after one cup of coffee, Jim Alter had diarrhea. He was sick for two days.

The group mostly stayed down at the beach, swimming in the ocean, meeting the row boats that came in every morning with fresh clams and crabs. It was a lazy and relaxed time. This group was so compatible that they continued to travel together.

Six months after their first trip, another couple, Herman and Janice Perez, Jimmy's in-laws, joined the group for a trip to Branson, Missouri, to hear the country western singers and then on to New Orleans for the Cajun cuisine, dancing at Mulate's, and a stroll down Bourbon Street. It was there that Angie bought herself a fancy metal washboard to play along with some metal fingertip rings that acted as picks.

When the ladies on the balconies shouted down, "Flash for beads. Flash for beads!" Dillon and Herman popped open their snap button shirts and bared their chests; before long, they had at least 20 beaded necklaces around their necks.

They took a ride down the Mississippi River on a paddle boat and another ride through the Bayou to watch the Cajun boatmen make the alligators jump out of the water to grab marshmallows off a stick.

Their longest and most memorable trip was in 1993, driving over 10,000 miles all the way to Alaska. This time only Jim and Cathy, Jim and Leone, and Bill and Sybil came with them. They drove caravan style, using walkie-talkies to communicate with each other. Their vehicles were put on a barge to cross the Yukon, continuing on to drive over what was called "The Road at the Top of the World," from Canada into Alaska. Stopping at the top at the Chicken Creek Saloon, they ate pancakes and huge cinnamon buns. They went swimming in hot springs deep in the forest.

Everywhere they went, the scenery was spectacular. The sport was fishing for Sockeye Salmon. Thousands of salmon were swimming from the ocean, up the Kenai Peninsula to spawn and then die at their place of birth. Having brought all the canning and smoking equipment, the travelers spent the afternoons canning up their fish.

In Homer, they went fishing for Halibut. Leone caught the biggest one, a 150 pounder. Some days, Dillon didn't feel well enough to fish. He gave Angie lessons and praised her when she brought in her catch.

In Heider, they were told they could see brown bears up close by standing on the bank of a narrow river. The ranger instructed them to be very quiet. She told them that every afternoon, the bears ventured out of the woods to patrol the river for their evening meal. The bears would grab up a salmon, smell it, and throw it back if it was a male fish. They only wanted the eggs in the female fish, ripping open the belly. The ranger also told the spectators most bears were accustomed to seeing tourists standing so close on the bank, but there was one bear named Millie, that could get ornery. If she started up the bank, they should run as fast as they could. Everyone held their breaths, when the bear came out of the woods and began to eat. Dillon, with his perverse sense of humor, shouted out, "Bear, bear!" The tourists ran in all directions. He couldn't understand why Angie wasn't laughing with him. The ranger gave him a stern look.

After three months, they headed home. Alaska truly was the last frontier and God's finest creation.

Jim, Leone, Angie   Elmer and Virginia

(left) Bill, Sybil, Angie, (right) Janice and Herman

(above left) Angie and Cathy (above, right) Jim

Angie practicing on land, and her first catch

(left) Sybil canning the salmon, (right)Millie the ornery bear.

Piña Colada time

Swimming in the hot spring

Flowers for Angie

143

After so many years, it was time to sell the flower shop. Angie felt some sadness. She would miss interacting with the customers. When she designed flowers for someone, she became part of their family during weddings, babies, sickness and funerals. Now she mostly felt relieved from all the work. She was tired of the shop. The holidays had been brutal. She often worked all night to get orders done. Angie had decided a while back that when the flowers were not fun anymore, she'd give up the shop.

Dillon bought her a Judith Liber purse to celebrate her retirement. It was a red jeweled rose and would become the first of Angie's expensive collection of Judith Liber purses: one for every child and grandchild. Even the two grandsons got one to give to their future wives.

Angie then began a collection of old carousel horses. Again, she wanted one for everyone in the family. They were parked in the living room, down the hall, in the bathroom, in the bedroom, until Dillon suggested she give their children their horses now since the herd was getting too large. "I can't believe you of all people would spend that much money on damn wooden horses." Angie was never a spender, always the saver. The family even teased her by calling her tight fisted, but there were some things she liked and didn't mind spending on them, especially as mementos for her family.

Chapter 18

1999-2002

When it came time for Dillon's annual physical, a simple check-up was performed, sigmoidoscopy to check his colon.

Later that afternoon, he complained of severe pain. Angie called the doctor, but all he said was that it's just gas, "Tell him to walk around."

Dillon's pain continued and increased, but after another call to the doctor, he was told it was gas once again. Finally, late at night, he was doubled over in pain and Angie insisted he go to the hospital.

They admitted him immediately. His colon had ruptured and, because several hours had passed, he was full of fluids which had caused peritonitis. Earl and Vivian had come with them and were in shock when the doctor told Angie he would do his best to save Dillon's life. He told them that he would perform a colostomy and wash out his insides as best he could. The doctor's diagnosis made them realize how dangerous the situation was.

They stayed all night at the hospital until the early morning when the doctor came out to give the prognosis. Dillon was going to live; however, it would be a long time before they could reconnect his intestines. Angie called the kids and brought them up to date with what the doctor had told her.

No drain had been put in and as Dillon sat up the next morning, the pressure caused the newly closed incision to burst open with his intestines literally falling out into his hands. With his dry sense of humor, he casually asked his attendant, "What should I do with these, tuck them back in?"

The nurse on duty had never seen that happen. Shocked and shaking, her training kicked in and she began pouring water on Dillon, remembering that she had to keep the intestines wet. She continued to throw water until the doctor arrived. Soaking wet, Dillon was rushed back into surgery within ten minutes.

This time, they closed the long incision down his abdomen with metal clamps. Again, no drain was put in.

All throughout the day, fluids built up, causing Dillon's stomach to swell. Seeing that Dillon was choking, son-in-law Ken asked the nurse on duty to suction him. Having no experience with the suction tube, the nurse kept calling for a doctor.

Angie was out in the hall, paralyzed with fear, hearing call after call for a doctor; none came.

Hours passed. Dillon lost consciousness. Barely breathing, he was drowning in the bile backing up into his throat. Ken had seen and heard enough of the gurgling to know that something had to be done immediately. Grabbing the suction tube, he began to force it down Dillon's throat, commanding him to, "Swallow, swallow." The bile came up, spraying Ken, Dillon, the ceiling and the walls.

Finally, a doctor came. Dillon was rushed into the intensive care unit and intubated. He remained unconscious for two days and eventually brought back to his regular room.

The surgeon criticized Ken for taking over and performing a procedure.

Furious, but keeping calm, Ken answered, "Would you have had me watch him drown?"

The metal clamps were removed from Dillon's stomach. The doctor was worried he might inflate again so the incision was left wide open. With the wound exposed, Dillon would surely get a staph infection; he told the family to get Dillon out of the hospital and take him home. The hospital promised to send a nurse to the house every day to clean and dress the open wound until it was healed from the inside out.

An ambulance brought Dillon home on a gurney. He had to be kept flat on his back and could not get up. Ken came every day to empty the colostomy bag, rolling him slightly from side to side to avoid bed sores. He emptied the bed pan and helped Angie bathe him.

"Thank you, Jesus, for Ken," Angie would say many times a day.

Jimmy was squeamish and could not look at the wound. He cried to see his father suffer so. To help out, he took over all the yard work and the girls popped in everyday with a dessert and a visit or just to say "I love you Daddy."

Granddaughter Kristie offered to take him to her tattoo artist; she suggested Dillon get the backend of a chicken tattooed over the scar where his navel used to be.

Dillon was so happy to be home with the family all around him, especially his Angel. "Come here and just hold my hand. I need to touch you."

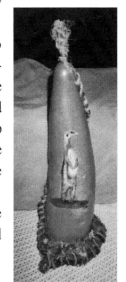

Angela wanted to be with him constantly, so she prepared vegetables for dinner or peeled tomatoes for canning while sitting on the bed beside him. She set up a table next to the bed. She had grown gourds in her garden that year and set up her paints there beside Dillon. The first gourd she painted was of a meerkat, one of Dillon's favorite animals.

Then she painted gourds for everyone in the family until the kids said, "Mom, stop. We all have enough gourds."

Angie then switched to painting on tiles or canvas. Dillon critiqued her work. He thought the funniest picture was one of the Grand Canyon with teepees and Indians sitting on the ground. "I think the Indians were smart enough to not pitch their teepees on the edge of the Grand Canyon," he laughed.

"What do you know, Dillon? It's called artistic license."

Never leaving his side, Angie sat with Dillon, laughing and talking, all day every day, while her beloved recovered. His sense of humor was one of the first things to come back.

True to their promise, the hospital sent a nurse every day for three months to wash out the long incision until it healed. The first nurse who came to the house was so short she didn't have to kneel on the floor to clean the wound. When the nurse left later that day, Dillon remarked, "She's so short, she could wear a top hat and walk under the belly of a horse." Angie just shook her head, always amused at his silly sayings.

The next nurse who reported for duty was a real beauty with humongous breasts. She would kneel on the floor and lean over Dillon while she changed his bandages, her breasts in his face. "Angie, save me! She's going to smother me."

"Oh, I bet you like it." Angie walked away with a laugh.

At the end of each day came a very modified love play. Angie kissed him and he licked her cheek. She'd snuggle close to him, holding his hand. Touching, touching, always touching.

 CR80

After three months, Dillon was beginning to heal enough that he could now slowly walk around.

Randy, the floral designer and friend, decided to come for a visit with her sister Vickie. Angie felt comfortable leaving Dillon for the day, so the women could go shopping in San Francisco and go see a play. Julie and Jill promised to look in on their father and fix him lunch.

Angie made Randy and Vickie promise to indulge her in something she always wanted to do; puzzled, they agreed.

"Just bring your camera," Angie told them. "I want a video."

Parking in the garage at Union Square, Angie went to the trunk of her car and brought out the metal washboard she had bought on Bourbon Street in New Orleans. She hung it on her shoulders and adjusted the metal fingers on her hands. "Randy, you bring the boom box and, Vickie, get that hat. Don't forget the camera. I'm going to be a street musician!" Angie revealed. "This is my day to shine."

Randy and Vickie exchanged looks, "I don't think she's kidding. Get the camera."

Her friends kept an eye out, waiting for a policeman to leave Union Square, and then proceeded to set up the boom box and put out the hat for donations.

Angie began to play along to a zippy Cajun tune, running her metal fingers up and down the washboard, keeping time with the music. She then began to dance around in a circle while she played another song, the fringe on the metal fingers flapped while she danced.

Soon a crowd had gathered around Angie. Off to the side, a homeless man started forward and began working her crowd.

What nerve, Angie thought and she sauntered over to him as she kept playing. "Would you mind terribly to wait until I'm through?"

Surprised, the man stepped back and sat down with the crowd.

Randy, seeing how Angie was enjoying herself, leaned over to Vickie and said, "We're never going to get her out of here."

149

Angie played three more songs before taking a bow. The crowd clapped and dropped coins in her hat, which Angie gave to the homeless man.

Still exhilarated from her performance and still wearing the washboard, Angie carried the boom box into Neiman Marcus. The saleslady tactfully asked, "Would you like me to keep your things behind the counter while you shop?"

Angie then bought another Judith Liber purse for $4,500.

Leaving Neiman Marcus, they returned the washboard and boom box to the trunk of the car and hurried over to the Orpheum Theater to see Phantom of the Opera. Angie fell in love with the Phantom and decided to buy Dillon a half mask and a black cape. She fantasized, *Maybe when he gets well, he can be my phantom.*

Back home, Julie and Jill almost wept with joy and relief. "Thank you. Thank you for taking her to Union Square." they told Randy and Vickie. "We were dreading it."

Randy and Vickie

෫෨

Many months later, the doctors were finally ready to reconnect Dillon's intestines, but first his carotid artery had to be cleaned out. One side was normal; the other side was 95% blocked. Back to the hospital he went.

It should have been a simple procedure, but with Dillon, nothing was every simple. During surgery, the nerve to his tongue, that was located beneath the carotid artery, was severed. This made eating and swallowing a slow and painful experience.

Not wanting Angie to worry anymore, Dillon told her, "I can live with this."

He rarely complained, just so grateful to be up and around. He got cranky sometimes, but Angie could make him happy with a kiss, calling him her loveable grouch. Still, they were touching, touching, always touching.

After the final surgery to reconnect the intestines, life seemed to return to normal. They began going out two or three times a week to the San Martin Café for breakfast. Two women, former truck drivers, ran the restaurant; Blanche and Gertrude had a specialty of chile verde with eggs, however, they had no skills with something as simple as pancakes. Customers sometimes teased that their flapjacks were as flat as tortillas. This always got the patrons laughing.

It was a place where people gathered to enjoy exceptional chile verde, but also a place to visit with each other and hear the town gossip. Dillon, having lived all his life two miles down the road from the café, socialized with everyone. Angie was happy to get out of cooking breakfast.

Dillon was feeling so well, he began to sing in the shower again. Angie enjoyed sitting in the bedroom, listening, even though his lyrics could get raunchy. He would begin singing something spiritual like "Jesus kicked me through the goal post of life," then to the extreme "two more women I'd like to ride are a coal black honey and a Cherokee hide."

If he knew Angie was listening in the bedroom, he switched to,
"You are so beautiful to me,
Can't you see?
You're everything I've ever hoped for.
You're everything I need.
You are so beautiful to me."

Her heart melted when he sang his love songs to her.

Coming out of the shower, Angie could see that familiar mischievous grin. "You want to try to slay the dragon?"

In seconds, she was wrapped around him like a raspberry vine.

He put up a mighty effort but he couldn't finish the job. "Angel, you might as well kill me now. I don't want to live a day longer."

"Oh, shush, you silly man. You've been sick a long time. Don't be so hard on yourself? Have you forgotten you're 68 years old?"

At the next doctor's appointment, Angie asked the doctor if Dillon could be given just a little Viagra.

"Jesus, woman, are you trying to kill him? He needs rest, not sex."

So they contented themselves with cuddling, caressing, petting, and touching, always touching: a repeat of their youthful dating years.

Just when Dillon was really gaining some strength, they got a call from the chief of surgery to come in for a conference.

Angie, Dillon, and Jimmy went to the hospital and met with him in his office, not knowing the reason. There were two other doctors present. After introductions were made, the chief bluntly said, "Mr. McCandless, you need immediate surgery."

Angie and Dillon looked at each other and almost started laughing. "You might as well give up being a doctor and learn how to clean crap out of a cuckoo clock, 'cause you're not ever going to get me in here again!"

"Mr. McCandless, be serious. Listen to me. You need immediate surgery!"

Jimmy recognized one of the doctors as the surgeon who had operated on Dillon's carotid artery and severed the nerve to his tongue. He also recognized him from the local paper as having just been charged with a DUI.

Softly, but with menace in his voice, he asked directly to that doctor, "Did you operate on the wrong side of my father's throat?"

The chief of surgery answered for him, "Yes. We did."

Angie felt a scream bubble up. She could hardly breathe. *This can't be happening. No more—he can't take anymore.*

Dillon calmly looked at the doctor and asked, "You want another crack at me?"

Jimmy jumped out of his chair. He put both of his hands down on the table and leaned forward and got right in the doctor's face. "You will never touch my father again."

The chief of surgery, trying to bring calmness back to the room, spoke up again, "I know this is a shock, but you have had two heart attacks and you have an artery that is still 95% blocked that needs attention. Now! You can have any surgeon you want and go to any hospital you want. We'll cover the cost."

They chose Stanford Hospital, the finest research hospital on the west coast, 45 miles north of Morgan Hill. On the day of the surgery they drove in silence. It was just Dillon and Angie in the car.

Finally Dillon said, "Pray for me, Angel. I can't think of any words."

For the first time, she saw a flicker of fear, so unlike his usual bravado. She prayed aloud for a good surgeon, a strong heart, and a quick recovery.

Dr. Taylor met them in the lobby. "Let's sit here a minute and talk. Then we'll take you up to your room." He began, "Mr. McCandless…"

"Dillon will do."

"Alright, Dillon. I've been reading your records. You're a walking miracle. There's a bit of a risk for you to have another surgery, so I'd like to keep you here for a few days and beef you up with vitamins and things before I get you in the cutting room. Is that alright with you?" He asked this with a smile, noticing their tension and wanting to make the atmosphere more relaxed. He knew he had succeeded.

Dillon smiled back with one of his off-the-wall sayings: "Well, shit and kick it, Doc. Have at me. I'm ready for your artwork. Make sure it's pretty.

Dr. Taylor knew the last doctor who operated on Dillon. He also knew of his drinking problem. As he was walking away, he turned around. Holding his hands out in front of him, palms turned down and wanting to reassure his patient, he called out, "Hey Dillon. See? My hands are steady. I don't drink."

They settled Dillon in his room with a TV and tubes going everywhere. "Angel, come here, sit close to the bed, so I can hold your hand. You know, you're all the courage I've ever needed. Did I tell you today that I love you with all my heart?"

"Yes Dillon. You tell me that every day, but you can tell me again and again."

"Angel, thank you for being my wife."

The surgery went well and Dillon was soon back home in the backroom watching TV and tinkering with all his stuff. He had a fetish for gluing things back together: an old cookie jar with a broken lid, statues of Abraham Lincoln and Venus de Milo, both with their heads lopped off. If he could find arms, he probably would have glued them on Venus.

The yard had various items too: a Mexican statue sitting under a cactus wearing a cracked sombrero, all the broken pieces carefully glued back together. There was a carved wooden statue of St. Isadore, the patron saint of farmers, with a shovel in his hand. One of his eyes had fallen out and Dillon teased Angie that she was the only person who owned a one eyed patron saint, but like magic, the next day St. Isadore had a leather patch placed over his empty eye socket.

Early in the morning, Dillon hand watered the back yard. When frogs came out for a drink, Angie would smile hearing the strange ribbit noises. If someone asked, she explained, "That's just Dillon, talking to his frogs.

In September of 2002, a new semester would soon start at Gavilan, the local community college. Angie wanted to take a painting class, so Dillon surprised her with a cart on wheels to hold her paints and canvas. The bigger surprise was that he wanted to go with her. He wasn't interested in painting, but he enjoyed pencil sketching cartoon characters. He audited the class and thought he could pick up a few pointers.

Angie suspected that he just wanted to be with her. She was always in his sight, 24-7, joined at the hip.

He smiled as he told her, "Imagine at my age, I'm going to be a college boy."

Still puttering around the garage, Dillon built Angie a prayer bench, fashioned from a picture he saw of Grandmother Savio's. "Now you can be comfortable when you pray for me." He built new planter boxes for Angie's herbs and a new dog house for Daisy, the little rat terrier that Jill bought him—Everyone thought a dog would be a good companion for him.

He put together a repair box for Angie. In it, he put a hammer, some nails, a screw driver, duct tape, and various other items. He placed it on the bottom shelf in the kitchen. "Now you know where to find these things you may need." He seemed to be tying down all the loose ends.

Chapter 19

2004-2005

Almost daily, Dillon and Angie went for rides that always ended up somewhere along the coast. His favorite places to eat were at the mouth of the ocean at Moss Landing Harbor or on the Monterey Wharf. He talked and talked, telling Angie old stories that she had heard fifty times. Sometimes she read a book while he drove and told his stories. On days when she didn't seem to be paying attention, Dillon would mumble, "I might as well buy a parrot to talk to," sounding like his feelings were hurt. She then put the book away, snuggled close to him, and put her hand on his leg or sometimes rest her head on his leg. Touching, touching, always touching. Oh, how she loved him.

On one particular sunny afternoon drive, Dillon spotted a boat for sale, a big boat, forty feet long. "It has a great engine room and can sleep five." Dillon explained excitedly.

Angie knew he would never be able to maneuver that monster boat out in the ocean but if it made him happy she would never say no to Dillon. The hospital had offered a settlement for all the mistakes they had made so they took it and bought the boat. Angie felt he earned it. He named it "La Chuparosa". Jimmy trailered it home and parked it in their driveway.

Dillon wore his skippers hat, climbed the ladder and sat up high in the wheel house dreaming of the day he and Angie would sail out to sea a couple of miles, cut the motor, drop anchor and just drift up and down on the waves. He visualized Angie sun bathing naked on the deck while he fished. He told her that's what they would do.

Dillon's remarks sparked a long ago memory. Angie though back to when they were young. To her and Dillon, there was nothing more glorious that being out in the middle of the ocean on a sunny day. It made her feel like they were all alone in the world. Dillon fished and Angie sun bathed naked on a bench.

Luckily, Dillon heard the put, put, put of a small boat approaching. "Angel, you might want to go into the cabin. Here comes Hector." Hector Valdez was his fishing buddy. He often took his little dinghy out to meet Dillon.

Angie gasped and rolled onto the floor and crawled into the cabin. Hector checked out Dillon's catch and then began to discuss the best locations to fish, the better fish to eat, recipes for fish, new lures to use, etc. He went on and on, while Angie shivered, hidden in the cool cabin.

Angie smiled to herself, thinking about those days and Dillon's suggestion. "Dream on Dillon. I am 65 years old! You know I'd never lie around naked anymore." He could always make her laugh.

"You still look beautiful to me, the same as when I first met you, with just a few extra pounds." He quickly added, "All in the right places." He could charm the snake out of the Garden of Eden.

⚜

When Dillon's 70th birthday was approaching, Angie began planning. She invited everyone they knew, family, old school friends, fishing buddies, new AA members: the eclectic group of people that filtered through his life.

The first year they were married she had given him a big surprise birthday party. Her family always made a big deal out of birthdays and she thought he would love a party, but after the surprise, Dillon begged her not to ever do that again. He hated being the center of attention. It hurt Angie's feelings that he didn't appreciate her hard work until she realized for the first time what a private and shy person he really was. Would she ever understand him? She loved him so and wanted to be the perfect wife, so she never threw him another party.

This year it was different. When she mentioned it, Dillon agreed to help her with the guest list. He was looking forward to seeing all the people who mattered to him.

Angie wanted this to be special for everyone. The party was held at Jim and Christie's house. Over 70 people said they were coming. All the kids spent the day setting out furniture and decorating the tables.

Angie made huge pots of crab cioppino with garlic bread and big bowls of leafy green salad. After so many years, she finally felt like she had mastered her mother's cooking. Antipasta plates of cheese, crackers, salami and olives were placed on each table.

She hired two men for entertainment. They played a guitar and a mandolin and sang for those that wanted to dance out on the patio. Huge heaters were placed around the yard, keeping it warm and cozy.

Dillon made the rounds, talking and visiting with everyone. He opened each present carefully, always having a funny comment for what he opened, especially the gag gifts. His sense of humor was in fine form and he kept the people laughing.

He was genuinely enjoying all the attention, but soon tired out and asked Angie if they could leave early. She could see how exhausted he was, but with a little encouragement, he managed to make one more round to thank everyone for coming and say goodbye.

Angie wondered to herself if he would see his 71st birthday.

CR80

Several times a day Dillon needed to lay down to rest. Barely a month had passed since the party, but he seemed to be struggling so much more. Angie knew he liked her near, so she never went too far.

One afternoon he called out to her, "Angel, come here and lie on top of me. I'm so cold. I'm shaking like a dog passing a peach pit."

She could see the blankets moving and noticed his flushed face. She rushed over, pressing her cheek against his forehead. "Dillon, you're going into the emergency room. You have a high fever."

After taking x-rays, nurses settled him into a hospital room and hooked him up with IVs and tubes.

Dillon heard the doctor talking to Angie. "He has pneumonia, viral pneumonia. Antibiotics won't help. His body will have to fight this off."

The doctor's greater concern was the spots they saw on his lungs. "It looks like one lung will have to be removed. We can't schedule the surgery until he's stronger. We'll just have to wait and see how he does in the next few weeks."

Earl and Vivian came to see him. They had been with him through so many of his hospital trips. This just seemed to be another. They stayed for a while and tried to cheer him up.

Dillon was sitting on the side of the bed when the nurse came in with a wheel chair. Smiling cheerfully, she said she was there to take him down to physical therapy. Stubbornly he answered back, "No, I don't believe you will," and he lay down.

The doctor came in regularly over the next few days to check his vital signs, seemingly unconcerned with his progress. Dillon's condition didn't seem to be getting any better.

"Angel, I'm so tired. I'm so blasted tired. Come hold my hand, just touch me," he said weakly. She stayed by his side day and night.

After some time, a nurse came in and motioned for Angie to follow her out to the corridor. She took her hand and said, "I'm going in there to wash and powder him all up so he'll smell real good. You go make your phone calls." She knew it was his time. So did Angie.

Several hours later, Julie and Jill were holding Dillon's hands on either side of the bed. He wanted to touch them. They raised his arms so he could place his hands on their cheeks. He said nothing, but looked at Julie with her brown eyes, so like her mother's, and Jill with her white blond hair so like his. *So beautiful*, he thought.

Angie pushed them aside. "Let him see me." Julie and Jill stepped out of the way. Dillon and Angie stared at each other for a long time just like they did at their first meeting. She was trying to memorize his every feature. He still had plenty of white blond hair; it was longer now, having given up the crew cut several years ago. His large mustache was pure white. She brushed her lips over his mouth and breathed out into him, telling him to not give her any trouble. "Please Dillon, I can't bear to see you struggle or gasp for air."

"I promise you. I won't"

With great effort, he haltingly whispered the words he had said to her almost every day of their marriage, "I love you with all my heart. Thank you for being my wife," and he closed his eyes.

Angie could see the heart monitor go to a flat line and knew Dillon had left her forever. She pulled all the tubes and lines out and lay down on top of him, wanting to touch all of him. The girls brought up his lifeless arms and placed them around her. He held her one last time. Angie nuzzled her head under his chin and kissed his neck. He smelled of soap and powder. Missing was the scent of his Old Spice.

Jimmy, who had been delayed getting to the hospital, came running into the room. Emotionally, he asked everyone to get out, "I need to talk to my pop." They graciously gave him time alone with Dillon. From outside in the hallway, they could hear him sobbing and talking softly.

After spending time together in the room, it was time for the family to leave him. Without thinking and true to her life-long thrifty nature, Angie picked up two of the unopened cartons of milk on his hospital tray and walked out.

Loretta Wilson

The nurse met her at the door and handed her a passage from the Bible, Ecclesiastes 3: 1-8, written by Solomon, King of Israel.

There is an appointed time for everything. And there is a time for every event under heaven—

A time to give birth and a time to die;
A time to plant and a time to uproot what is planted.
A time to kill and a time to heal;
A time to tear down and a time to build up.
A time to weep and a time to laugh;
A time to mourn and a time to dance.
A time to throw stones and a time to gather stones;
A time to embrace and a time to shun embracing.
A time to search and a time to give up as lost;
A time to keep and a time to throw away.
A time to tear apart and a time to sew together;
A time to be silent and a time to speak.
A time to love and a time to hate;
A time for war and a *time for peace.*

It was Dillon's time to die.

Morning Tide
January 4, 1935

Evening Tide
February 23, 2005

෬෩

Angie had yet to cry. There was so much to do. She contacted Habing Family Funeral Home, and they arranged for a bagpiper to play "Amazing Grace" out at the cemetery. Brother-in-law Dale, the seminary man, would give the final prayer there. She reminded Jim Habing, the funeral director, to cut a little piece of Dillon's hair for her. Jacob had given her a piece of his baby hair, now she wanted a piece of his old man hair. Surprisingly, the pieces were still the same color; white blond.

Dillon had asked her to give the eulogy. "I know how you like microphones. It will be your best performance. Then they'll be looking at you instead of me in the casket." A plain pine box would be Dillon's final resting bed; nothing flashy or shiny.

As she picked out his burial clothes and laid them on the bed, Daisy, his dog, jumped up and settled on top of them. "You miss him too, don't you girl?" Angie asked sadly, as she petted the little dog.

Jimmy got out Dillon's old '63 Lincoln. He wanted to drive it to the funeral. It rained all that week and Jimmy had left

Dillon's dog Daisy, lying on his burial clothes

the car out of the garage the night before.

The next morning when Jimmy came to get the car, the horn began to honk on its own. A chilling thought occurred to them all.

"I never could get away with anything," cried Jimmy. "He caught me again, leaving the car out in the rain." They all laughed, remembering the time Jimmy had taken his father's truck without permission. When Dillon started up the truck the next day, the radio blasted out full volume. "How does he always know?" Jimmy smiled sadly. They spent all day together reminiscing about Dillon's antics.

When Angie sat down to write the eulogy, remembering was easier than she thought it would be. Instead of shedding tears, she laughed, remembering all of their adventures together. She and Dillon's life had been full of wonderful memories. Despite the hard times and the struggles they had, she couldn't help but smile as she wrote page after page, wanting the speech to perfectly share their memories, happy and not so happy, with Dillon's friends and family at the funeral. She wanted, needed, them to understand what Dillon meant to her.

The day before the funeral, Angie went to the store to buy all the groceries for the gathering after the funeral. As she stepped up on the front porch with two bags of groceries in her arms, she tripped and fell. The eggs were smashed, oranges rolled away, and everything else was strewn about. Finally overwhelmed with sadness, Angie laid down on the step, put her face on the concrete and began to cry, not just sobbing and tears, but mournful sounds like an animal, not realizing they were coming out of her.

Chapter 20

The night of the funeral, the room was packed. The overflow room was packed as well. The guests seated there could watch the ceremony on a big screen.

Angie walked slowly up to the podium. "I know this is a bit unusual for the wife to give the eulogy, but then again, Dillon was always a bit different. We talked freely about dying. He only wanted me to give his funeral service, because he didn't want anyone to tell 'all those lies' about how wonderful he was. He'd say 'Tell it like it was, with no puffery and don't embellish too much.'"

She took a deep breath and began to share their early history with the crowd. "I met Dillon when I was 16, though I lied and said I was 17. We met at the Santa Clara County fair. He liked to tell people that he had to go out of town to find me. I thought he was so handsome, wearing his Levi's and boots, his white blond hair flying."

"His friend, Tacci, sold him his first suit so he could take me to the prom: a blue one-button suit with the blue suede shoes of the 50s. Over the years, he would often ask me, 'would you marry me again?' and I'd wait awhile and then say 'yeah, I'd probably marry you again 'cause I loved your '52 blue Ford.'

Even when he was on crutches, he drove to San Jose to see me 3-4 times a week. And when I went off to college, he'd drive to Belmont on Wednesdays so we could visit for two hours. He'd pick me up on Friday afternoon and drive me back to school on Sunday night. After five months, we thought, 'This is silly. Let's just get married.' And the next month, we did. January 26, 1957. Dillon was terrified by all those people who came to our wedding. If it wasn't for Earl, I doubt he would have made it to the church."

"And so we began our married life. Living with Dillon was like being on a roller coaster, all ups and downs. After a couple of years, we began to have children, three babies in two and a half years. But I never worried that Dillon would fail to support us. He worked at Western Gravel for 25 years. On the side, he was always buying and selling something: boats, cars, trailers, whatever. He encouraged me to open the flower shop. Shortly after that, he began to need various surgeries. I tried to count up how many, well over 20. All the while, he helped me with the flower deliveries or the shop clean up whenever he could."

"Dillon could be a difficult man to live with. He was so compulsive that he did everything in excess. He could not buy just one of anything. He loved boats—the bigger, the better. I remember, once we had two 34' boats sitting side by side in the driveway. He would just sit there, in the driver's seat, like Skipper Sedley. A neighbor asked me if there was a flood coming that she should know about. She wanted to put cardboard waves around the boat. But then he'd sell them and something else would come in."

"When he smoked, he smoked too much and when he drank, he drank too much. He always credited our daughter Julie's eyes with convincing him to stop drinking. That was 28 years ago, and he never drank again, because he loved us. These last years were our very best years. He said he saved the best for last. We took vacations every year, in between the trips to the hospital. He cemented our family together, the people he loved best. But Dillon also loved the unlovable. He had a very eclectic group of friends. The worse their flaws, the more he loved them. He understood their hurting.

"The past five years, I pretty much put my life on hold. But what precious years they have been. Dillon wanted me and his family near.

And they always were near, dropping by every day. This meant so much to him."

As she spoke, Angie was reliving all their precious memories. Occasionally, a tear tolled down her cheek.

"He had one room in our house where he watched the History Channel. I called it 'the Junk Room,' because it had all his books, souvenirs, toy cars, and things arranged on every bookshelf. That was his inner sanctum. The grandchildren could come in, but not touch anything. When he was watching T.V, it would annoy me to no end when I'd be busy and he'd holler out 'Come here, come here, you gotta see this.' So go, I would, and he'd say, 'oh, you're too late.' He just wanted me to sit there with him, hold his hand, and talk and talk, and listen to his old stories again and again."

"We often went to Reno, and stayed at the Nugget casino. He had his second heart attack there. When the paramedics came, I heard them say 'eleven over zero, no pulse' and I was sure he had died, but like so many other times, he rallied around and as he was going out the door on the gurney, he yelled out 'Save my machine! I'll be right back!' Dillon was outrageous. His humor was strange and I usually had to interpret what he meant. Once we got back home from Reno, we would go for walks in the field across the road with his dog, Daisy, to try to get him stronger. We could see Murphy's Peak and across to the mountains and Finley Ridge. He thought we lived in the most beautiful place."

"About three weeks ago, I called the paramedics again. He had pneumonia, kidney problems, and another major heart attack while in the hospital. He would tell the doctors that with 'all those Catholics praying for him,' he couldn't die if he wanted to. He felt like all those prayers kept him alive, over and over. He appreciated them. Every day, I'd ask him if he would be alive tomorrow, but on the day he died he would not answer my question, because he always kept his promises to me. Every day for years he would say, 'Did I remember to tell you I love you with all my heart and thank you for being my wife?' and I would say, 'And well you should; no one else would have lived with you this long or loved you more.'"

"Somehow, we were all thinking and praying he could pull this off again. I was not ready to let him go. I prayed for a little more time. God, in his tender mercy, gave me another week. Dillon talked to me about his funeral. 'Don't put a necktie on me. Give them my old underwear. No fur balls on my socks.' He asked me to wear his shoes. I thought that was insane, but he explained that then I'd know he was with me. I promised him I would. See? I kept my promise." Angie lifted her foot to show the shoes.

"He was never afraid to die and said he would hold the Lord to His promise of a new body, since this one was falling apart. I need to tell you about his spirituality. When we were first married, being the good little Catholic girl I was, I baptized him when he was asleep. About 20 years later, he decided he wanted to be really baptized. Since he wasn't a churchgoer, he wanted me to baptize him in the hot tub. 'None of that Catholic sprinkling. I want the real thing, a real dunking.' He spoke of his Lord like He was his alone. He believed in his Savior. He loved to talk about the scriptures. We often teased him, 'here comes the gospel according to Dillon McCandless' He shared freely with anyone who would listen. So I am comforted by the scripture that says, 'I am the Resurrection and the Life. He who believes in me, though he is dead, shall live.'"

"Now let me end with his thoughts of his children and grandchildren:

Julie: He loved you for your tender, gentle ways, for listening to him when he wanted to talk.

Jill: Only Dillon called her "Willy." He loved that you came to the house and cut his hair, and, almost daily, you would pop in and kiss him with 'I love you, Daddy.'

Jimmy: He was so proud of you. When someone told him what a good kid you were, he would beam. He loved that you brought donuts every Sunday, and he would often say, 'No one has a finer son.'

Nick: You were his first grandchild. He loved your reserved ways, and he'd say 'That's one smart boy.'

Kristie: He loved you unconditionally—always telling her how beautiful she was. He even liked your tattoo.

Mackenzie: The quiet one. He would pick her up from school and try to get her to talk. 'How was school? What did you learn?' She'd give him one word answers. Then he'd tell me, 'She's almost a teen-ager.'

Colton: When you were told that Grandpa died, you said that you would have a hole in your heart. We all have that hole. He loved your football games, especially when the girls would chant, 'Colton, Colton' as you ran for a touchdown.

Sweet Stevie: She used to take naps with us. She would tickle his back, and he would giggle for her.

Alissa: The little princess—always so perfect and precise. He loved your beautiful pictures and drawings.

And then, Kacie: She gave him lots of fun. He loved her independent personality. He called her his little tornado.

Son-in-law Ken: They had more arguments than you could count. They loved to discuss theology and whenever Ken got too lofty, Dillon would say, 'There you go again using those big words—keep it simple. God is love.' Ken was extremely kind to Dad when he was sick—washing him and turning him over in the hospital bed to be more comfortable. Thank you, Ken.

Son-in-law Steve: I'm afraid Steve had a hard time being the only Democrat in the family. Dillon admired your work ethic. Thank you for being patient with him.

Daughter-in-law Christie: Christie is a jewel. He kept after her to give him another grandson, but she told him to get a pet, so Jill bought him Daisy, the terrier dog that just liked to sit on his lap all day."

(left) Dillon with Nick, (right) Kristie

Dillon and Angie with (from left) Mackenzie,
Colton, Alissa, Kacie and Stevie

"I wish I could tell you all the special thoughts he talked to me about—my sisters, my Ya-Ya friends, and others. He could tell funny stories about you all."

"But most of all, he loved me. He affirmed me. He made me feel beautiful. He always called me his little hummingbird. After we went to Mexico for a month, he changed it to 'La Chuparosa.' When our gardenia bush bloomed, he brought a fresh gardenia every day into our bedroom. Oh, he could be quite the romantic. Except the time when he bought me a tackle box for my birthday." The crowd laughed.

When it had quieted down again, Angie continued, "Dillon was fully awake before he died. I told him not to give me any trouble. I wanted no bad memories. He saw us all and we could still talk to him. When he had no more breath, I could still see his lips saying, 'I love you, I love you.' And then he went on his journey to Jesus."

"So now I say to him, 'I love you with all my heart. Thank you for being my husband.'" Then Angela began to sing—"*You take the high road and I'll take the ...*"

Suddenly, all the children and grandchildren gathered around her and started to sing with her, but she held up her hands. "You can sing with me the second time 'round. This first time, I must sing alone for my husband." She walked over to the casket. She leaned down and kissed Dillon's forehead. She held his hand, touching, touching, always touching, and began to sing.

"You take the high road,
And I'll take the low road,
And you'll get to Heaven before me.
For me and my true love
Will never meet again
On the bonnie, bonnie banks of Lock Lomond."

❧ *The End* ❦